JACOB PAYNE, BOUNTY HUNTER, VOLUMES 1 - 4

Western Adventures

A.T. BUTLER

CONTENTS

TROUBLE BY ANY NAME

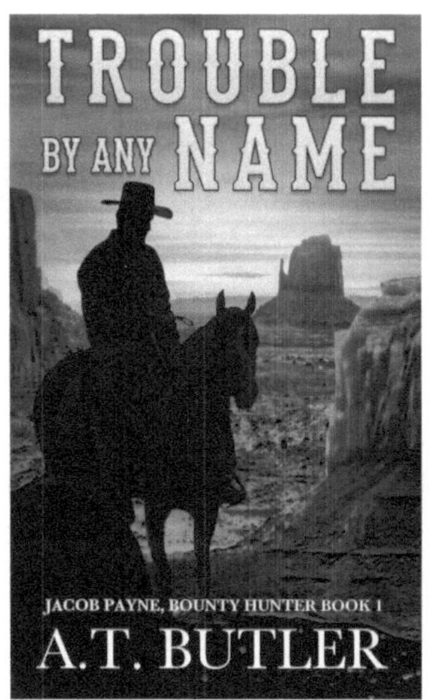

CHAPTER ONE

"I knew you'd get him, Payne," Sheriff Williams said.

When bounty hunter Jacob Payne handed over the stinking, nearly unconscious horse thief, the sheriff grabbed hold of the upper arms of the drunk before he fell on his face on the hard wooden floor. The older, heavyset man pushed and shuffled the thief back into one of the dirty cells of the Bennettsville jail before he came back out to give the bounty hunter his reward.

Jacob had turned to gaze out the window of the jail while he waited. His tall, built frame filled the entire window as he looked out, his dusty coat fitting snuggly over his broad shoulders. He watched the small town bustle. Shop owners stood in their doorways to greet passersby. Women in starched bonnets stopped to talk to their neighbors as they passed on the boardwalk. Small children pulled free of their mothers and ran out into the street, kicking up dust as they played and dodging horses. Bennettsville was a small town. Even from here Jacob could feel their affection for one another.

Jacob had learned of the reward and picked up the trail of the horse thief, Ted Glassey, outside Tucson. The trail was plain as day, as though it hadn't even occurred to Glassey that someone might try to follow him. He had only stolen a single horse, after all. Surely not worth the trouble for most bounty hunters. But Jacob Payne didn't get to be the best by turning up his nose at small rewards. Each new opportunity gave him a chance to learn, to get better, and to add more to his savings.

The thief's track had led Jacob to a dry riverbed a few miles outside Bennettsville. Glassey had built a fire. He was keeping it small, but not small enough to hide from Jacob, whose keen sense of smell was a unique advantage he had over other lawmen. It was that same unique advantage that drew him straight to the campfire. He tied his horse down fifty yards away and crept up to Glassey's camp on foot.

Once he got close enough, he saw he needn't have worried. Glassey was passed out drunk, whiskey bottle in hand. Without even having opened his bed roll. Jacob walked right up to the thief, pulled the bottle from his grasp, and bound his wrists without the other man even waking up.

Now that he had brought the prisoner back to town and secured the reward, Jacob could think about his next steps. His dark hair, almost black, was more shaggy than he was used to. Jacob made a mental note to visit the barber before he left town. It was easier to live rough without messy hair to fall in his face. But after that, he could be on his way. He'd find the next outlaw that needed to be taken down and make the country safer.

"He give you much trouble, Payne?" Sheriff Williams asked as he reentered the office.

Jacob shook his head. "Nope. The man was already passed out when I found him. Seemed surprise anyone came after him, to be honest. Thought he was better hidden in the brush than he really was. It was just a matter of getting him on his horse and in the direction of the jail."

"Easy money, sounds like."

"Sure. But I didn't come all the way to Arizona because it's easy."

Sheriff Williams nodded and lowered his bulk into the narrow wooden chair behind his desk. He rummaged in the bottom drawer, pulled out a sack of cash, and counted out the twenty dollars that was Jacob's due.

"You'll return the horse?" Jacob asked.

The sheriff nodded. "I'll take care of it, get word to them at the Triple S Ranch. Where will you go now? Not enough trouble in Bennettsville to tempt you, I'm guessing."

"Nope. You're doing a fine job here all on your own. I can be of more use somewhere else." Jacob examined the wall of wanted posters by the door. "What can you tell me about this'n?" He pointed to the dead-or-alive price for Elliott "Slippery" Stone. Three thousand dollars was a sizable reward.

Sheriff Williams shook his head. "Haven't heard head or tail of the Slippery Stone Gang in months.

Makes me nervous. Like they may be planning some-thing big. That one, though." He pointed to the next poster over. "Jeremiah Blanchard, with the five-hundred-dollar reward, I might have some info on. A few days ago there was a stranger come through here who claimed he saw a man fitting that description just up the road in San Adrian."

"You think that's true?"

Sheriff Williams leaned forward on the desk. "He seemed certain. The man said this was the new sheriff of San Adrian going by a different name."

"The sheriff?"

He leaned back in his chair, folding his hands over his belly. "Seems the last sheriff died and this new man up and took over a month or so ago. Stranger what came through here didn't say much else. Didn't seem to want to stay long, neither. Might be some trouble over in San Adrian even if this isn't your man."

"I'll check it out," Jacob said. He read over the poster's details. He'd be looking for a short man. Of course, most men were short compared to Jacob, but this Jeremiah character was barely over five feet. Dark hair beginning to gray. Scar along the man's left cheek. "Poster says he's wanted for murdering his wife and her parents. How'd such a despicable character make it all the way out here without getting caught?"

Sheriff Williams shook his head. "That's the way of it sometimes. It's why I became a lawman."

Jacob studied the drawing, committing the man's face to memory. "Says here he's from Virginia."

"You familiar with it?"

"Might be. Might have been there once. Feels like a long time ago, though."

"Might be useful for you."

"Might be. Did this stranger say what the new name was?"

"Horne. Sheriff John Horne. He ain't been there that long, but this ain't the first time I've heard stories come out of that town."

"All since the last sheriff died?"

Williams nodded. "Seems to be more good folk leaving there than going. If this new sheriff is a murderer, that might explain some of their unease."

Jacob raked his eyes over the other wanted posters lining the wall by the door. All the known members of the Slippery Stone Gang, of course, but also a motley collection of murderers, bank robbers, smugglers, rapists, and all manner of bad men running loose. Many people might look down on bounty hunters, call them killers or profiteers and sneer at them for taking money to kill people, but Jacob didn't see it that way. He was just one more member of law enforcement. If he took a bigger financial reward than a sheriff or U.S. Marshal, it's because he took a bigger risk as well.

As was the case now. Jacob was about to head into a dangerous situation, all on his own, with only his revolver and his wits to defend him.

"Well, it seems I have an appointment with Sheriff Horne, then," Jacob said. "Appreciate your help and the info."

"Glad to," Sheriff Williams said. "You've been a great help to me, not having a deputy. Next time you're in Bennettsville, you're welcome. I'll buy you a drink."

Jacob tipped his hat in thanks as he went out the door. He tucked his twenty dollars deep in his pocket and strode off to find the tonsorial parlor before his several-hour ride to San Adrian.

CHAPTER TWO

Jacob guided his pinto along the twelve miles to San Adrian. He kept one eye on the horizon and one eye on the brush. Snakes, scorpions, and tarantulas would usually stay away from horses out here in the desert, but Jacob followed the wisdom that you never could be too careful.

The sun was climbing in the sky. Jacob had plenty of water and turned his attention to the task ahead of him.

He needed to consider his plan of attack. In his last nine months of bounty hunting, nearly all of his targets had either fought back and shot at him once they realized they had been caught, or gave themselves up and hoped to live another day. This time could be different. This time his target had already spent weeks to get the town on his side and could lean on that new alliance to escape. Jacob would have to break that link.

As he rode into San Adrian later that morning,

Jacob felt the unsettling chill of a town under pressure. There was a muted quality about it, like the weight of a heavy quilt tamping down the town's energy. Hardly anyone was out in the street, unusual for the lunch hour when he arrived and a stark contrast to Bennettsville earlier that day. The few citizens that were outside kept their heads down, watching their feet, not making eye contact with Jacob or with each other. He didn't even try to say hello.

Not very sociable, he thought to himself. No wonder people are leaving this place.

He trotted slowly up the center of the main thoroughfare in San Adrian, toward the brick hotel at the end of the street. No friendly waves or neighborly greetings found him along the way. It was as though the citizens of the town didn't want to be seen, like they were hiding from something.

Or someone.

At the end of the main street stood the Wildflower Hotel, the tallest building in town at three stories. Jacob tied up his horse outside and made his way in.

The lobby was deserted this time of day. An older woman met Jacob at the counter. A small, ludicrously feathered hat sat atop her tight gray curls. Jacob wondered if the woman's aim was to be memorable or if she just didn't realize how ridiculous the thing truly was.

"Good morning, ma'am. You have a room available tonight?"

She glanced over his shoulder toward the front

door. "You may call me Mrs. Finch. I might find something for you. What business do you have in San Adrian? How long do you think you'll be here?"

Jacob shrugged. "A day or two. I've got business with the new sheriff. Horne, I think I heard his name was."

Mrs. Finch pursed her lips. She didn't comment but paused before she pulled out her ledger for Jacob to sign in.

Jacob noticed her hesitation. "Beg your pardon, Mrs. Finch, but I've never met the new sheriff. Is there anything I should know?"

She visibly relaxed after that, and she handed Jacob the pen. "Oh, well, that's all right then. We've had all kinds come through here these last few weeks, all looking for Sheriff Horne and all making trouble during the time they're here. I thought you might be one of them."

"No, ma'am. I apologize for worrying you. I was sent here by the sheriff of Bennettsville to look into a couple things. What kind of trouble you been having?"

"All kinds. Cheatin' at cards, putting wild stories in the ears of some of the boys around here, harassing poor women just trying to do their shopping. If he weren't the sheriff, I might think Mr. Horne was trying to take over this town, the way his friends seem to be scaring everyone away from San Adrian."

Jacob kept what he knew to himself. This Horne fellow wasn't a sheriff. Not really.

"Do you know he has four deputies now?" Mrs.

Finch shook her head. "Four. Never before has San Adrian needed such firepower. I've not seen the like."

"Has anyone talked to him about these new strangers coming into town?"

"Well, my husband tried. Mr. Finch owns this hotel, you know. One of the most important men in town, of course." She leaned forward conspiratorially. "But he didn't want to make more trouble. When the sheriff threatened him with his pistol and told Mr. Finch to mind his own business, he dropped it. And if Sheriff Horne's new friends all stopped staying here? We'd be out of business. Besides, it's hard to tell a man he's doing wrong when he's wielding a gun and surrounded by four armed deputies."

Jacob filed this information away. He would have to come up with a way to get Sheriff Horne on his own. He didn't want to have to fight his way through a crowd of men all armed and deputized to uphold their bastardized version of the law.

"Thank you very kindly, Mrs. Finch. I'll keep all that in mind. I wonder if I could trouble you for one more thing. Can you tell me where I might get lunch around here?"

"Well, I can set you up with some biscuits and jerky to take with you, but if you'd like a hot meal then the best place is Ed's saloon up the road a bit. We used to have a proper diner, but Sally packed up and moved north after just a couple weeks of dealing with Sheriff Horne's men." She shook her head again.

"Think I passed the saloon on my way here. Ed? He the owner?"

Mrs. Finch nodded. "Ed Baker owns the place and

tends the bar. His wife cooks, but they only serve food at meal times, so you'd best hurry and get over there before lunch is over. The Bakers have lived here as long as San Adrian's been standing, but things have got so bad, even Ed is talking about pulling up stakes."

Jacob thanked the hotel proprietress and said his good-byes. He led his horse to the livery and paid for food and stabling for a couple days. He didn't know how long he'd need to stick around to capture Blanchard, but the pinto could take a well-earned rest while he was in town. Next, Jacob sought out his hot lunch. Without crowds of people or gregarious shopkeepers trying to get his attention, he had no trouble finding the saloon just a few blocks east of the hotel.

When he entered, everyone in the room turned to look. At the sight of a stranger some of the customers just turned away again, but three or four took the time to glare at him, turn a cold shoulder and do whatever they could to make him feel unwelcome without making trouble. He could understand it. From their perspective, he was just one more stranger come to descend on San Adrian and wreak havoc.

"Y'all got coffee?" Jacob asked as he sat down at the bar across from its tender, a bald older man with a salt-and-pepper beard.

"Give me a few minutes and I'll make you a fresh pot."

"Thanks. You Ed? Name's Jacob Payne. Mrs. Finch sent me, said you'd be serving lunch about this time."

Ed nodded. "You almost missed it, but I'll have my wife fix you a plate. Anything else?"

"No, sir. Not right now."

Ed left to start the coffee, and Jacob turned his attention to the rest of the saloon's patrons. He was the only one sitting at the bar, but diners sat at more than half the room's tables. Jacob felt as if the other customers, mostly men, were watching him, waiting for him to give some kind of clue as to his loyalties or his business. The room was full of chatter, but Jacob couldn't make out any individual conversations.

A few minutes later, Ed came back out to the bar, hands full with a plate of roasted chicken and potatoes and a cup of coffee. It smelled delicious and Jacob heard his stomach growl. He was used to it; he often went without meals while on the road, so focused on tracking down criminals as he was.

Ed set the plate and mug down in front of Jacob, then stepped a short distance away and started wiping down dirty glasses. He glanced at Jacob every few seconds as he did so, as though wary he might try something.

"Where can I find Sheriff Horne?" Jacob asked as he took his first bite of hot, buttery potatoes. He kept his voice down. He didn't know who any of the other customers were. One might be the outlaw's right-hand man.

"Well," Ed started slowly. "If you hadn't told me Mabel Finch had sent you, I might not be willing to say. I don't like to get on the sheriff's bad side. But as far as I know, he might be comin' here tonight for supper or cards. That's the best I can offer you. Says he has a lot of cleaning up to do after Sheriff Winthrop died. Paperwork or some such. He stays shut inside the jail most days."

"Really?" Jacob took a drink of his coffee.

Ed nodded, keeping his attention on the dusty mug under his rag. "No one's really sure what he's doing there, but your best bet if you want to go find him is to show up at the jail."

"Thanks for the tip."

Jacob took his time finishing his chicken and potatoes, all the while watching the other customers in the saloon. To a man, they all looked cowed. The chatter that filled the room wasn't the cheerful, sociable conversations he expected to hear over lunch. They were frantic, whispered discussions, hurried meals so the men and women could leave again quickly. He put down a dollar for his meal and drink and strode through the door.

Time to find the man going by the name Sheriff Horne.

CHAPTER THREE

All the shutters of the San Adrian jail were closed, blocking out the world. No light shone inside; no hint of movement. Jacob hadn't seen anyone so much as walk by this part of the street. Since he'd first arrived, the afternoon sun had sunk from high in the sky to halfway down to the horizon, softly warming his weather-worn face.

For nearly three hours the bounty hunter stood across the street and watched the building. He was used to waiting. Many times, on a tracking, he would have to sit for days waiting for a target to show themselves. This time, though, he had a full belly and a shady spot to wait. It felt almost too easy.

For the last few hours, Jacob saw no movement nor even a hint that the building was occupied. Finally, he started to consider the possibility that it wasn't. Maybe he had been waiting outside an empty building this whole time. Maybe he was wrong and this so-called sheriff was out there doing good, making an arrest or saving a child from a well.

Then Jacob reminded himself of Jeremiah Blanchard's crimes. A man who would murder a woman in cold blood wouldn't be taking his time to help any child. A man on the run all the way from Virginia wouldn't waste his time serving San Adrian's citizens. Jacob just needed to lay eyes on Sheriff Horne, confirm it was the same man going by a different name, and make his arrest.

The bounty hunter hoped it would be as easy as that. He always tried to take his targets alive when possible, but if a man pointed a gun at him it was either kill or be killed.

And Jacob wasn't aiming to be killed.

Just as he was beginning to think he had wasted his afternoon and should give up to try somewhere else, the front door of the jail opened. Three men walked out onto the wooden boardwalk.

At this distance, Jacob couldn't hear what they were saying but could read their gestures sure enough. The shortest one seemed to be the man in charge. He was bearded with long, dark hair showing streaks of gray. He didn't even bother to pull his hat down to hide his face. Jacob saw immediately that this was Jeremiah Blanchard. The other two men seemed to be listening to Blanchard give them instructions, leaning their heads in deference to him.

None of the three noticed the bounty hunter watching them from just across the street. It wasn't until a fourth and fifth man exited the building that any of the group noticed Jacob. The tallest of the men looked both ways up and down the street. Since nearly all the other citizens of the town were avoiding being seen outside, Jacob was impossible to miss, casually leaning against the wooden side of the building opposite the jail.

The tall man pointed at Jacob and yelled. "You! What do you want? Don't you have anywhere else to be?"

Jacob stepped away from the building and pushed his coat back so Jeremiah and the deputies could see his weapon. He took a few steps forward until he stood in the middle of the dusty street. The men remained on the boardwalk in front of the jail.

"Afternoon, gentlemen. I'm hoping you can help me. I'm looking for Jeremiah Blanchard."

The sheriff's expression got hard, his eyes like coal, his teeth all but bared. Now that he was close, Jacob was even more sure this was the man he sought. There was the scar trailing the left side of his face, clear as day.

One of the deputies, the oldest one wearing an all-white beard, similarly tried to stare Jacob down. He slowly drew his weapon from its holster—not yet pointing it at Jacob, but ready. That gun made Jacob think twice about capturing Jeremiah then and there. As he'd expected, Blanchard wouldn't make this easy.

The other three deputies seemed plainly confused by this stranger in the street.

"Don't know anyone by that name," one said. "What's your business with him?"

"What about you, boys? Deputy Barnes, Deputy Conroy?" the sheriff asked the older man who had drawn his gun and the tall, barrel-chested man. "Does that name sound familiar to you? You ever heard of a Jeremiah Blanchard?"

They shook their heads but kept their eyes on Jacob.

"He's wanted for murder in Virginia," the bounty hunter said, "and I got a tip he might've made it all the way out here."

"Murder?" asked the young, lanky deputy.

Jacob nodded and turned his attention to the alleged sheriff. "Murdered his wife and her elderly parents."

Deputy Conroy spit and shook his head. "What's this man look like?"

Jacob paused, acting like he had to think about it. Best not show all his cards. Not yet. "Short. Dark hair with gray in it. You have his wanted poster? It'd be a lot easier than me trying to describe him."

"What's the matter, you deaf?" Deputy Barnes asked. "Ain't we just told ya we ain't heard that name?"

"Huh," Jacob said, deliberately casual. "And you're sure you didn't see that name on any of the wanted posters in there? That seems strange. Woulda thought at least news that the bastard's wanted would get out to San Adrian, even if *he* didn't."

"Look, Mister . . . ?" Sheriff Horne began.

"Payne," Jacob supplied. He strolled closer to his target, showing the man he wasn't afraid.

"Mr. Payne. We appreciate your concern. But as you might have heard, I've only recently taken over as sheriff of this town. What my predecessor might've done with that particular wanted poster I cannot say."

"You're telling me you lost a wanted poster? What happens if someone comes in with his body? How will you identify him?"

The man shrugged. "If that happens, we can figure it out then. I tell you, it's a mess around here. Haven't even had time to look over those posters myself. But I can look for you. Jonathan Blanch, you said?"

"Jeremiah. Blanchard." Jacob spoke with exaggerated diction. "From Virginia. Y'all ever been there?"

Sheriff Horne smiled menacingly. "Can't say I have."

Can't say, or *won't say*? thought Jacob.

"Beautiful place, Virginia," Jacob said, smiling back. "Man must've done a terrible thing to get over leaving that paradise and make it all the way out here to hide in this parched country."

"Well, of course, anyone could say the same thing about you or me, Mr. Payne. Tell me, what are you doing here in the Territory of Arizona?"

Jacob shrugged. "This and that. I've my reasons for leaving back east. None of them are murder, though."

There was a heavy pause as the bounty hunter and sheriff exchanged threatening glares.

"I think you've wasted enough of our time, Mr. Payne," Sheriff Horne said finally. He rested his hand on the butt of his gun but didn't draw it; the implication that he could was enough. He stayed on the boardwalk, which made a man of his height just tall enough to look Jacob in the eye. "I'd hate to have to run you out of town for being a menace to my citizens."

Jacob held the sheriff's gaze as he backed away. He didn't need to be told twice. He'd retreat for now so he could come up with a better plan for cornering his prey. As long as the man kept pretending to be Sheriff Horne, Jacob knew there would be another chance to take down Jeremiah Blanchard.

CHAPTER FOUR

Jacob was almost back to the hotel when someone came calling.

"Wait—mister!" Jacob heard from behind him. "Mr. Payne? Wait, I want to talk to you."

He turned to see a tall, gangly blond kid running up the street. He couldn't be any older than fifteen, but carried a Navy Revolver probably older than he was and had a shiny deputy's badge pinned securely to his front.

When Jacob saw it was the young deputy, he put his hands up, away from his holsters. "Look, I agreed to leave you fellas alone for now. You gotta do the same."

"No, you got it wrong." The kid stopped before him, breathing hard. "I was deputy to Sheriff Winthrop before he died. Name's Timothy Brady. I'm not with those guys. That's what I want to talk to you about."

Jacob lowered his hands and looked over the kid carefully. He had a snub nose, and still a lot of the child about his face. But Jacob could also see the beginnings of worry lines forming between the youth's eyebrows, as though every day was more stressful than the last for him. As though he'd been forced into adulthood before he was ready. Brady's eyes looked worried yet hopeful. Jacob knew he should at least talk to the kid.

"Well, in that case, let's talk. Maybe we can help each other."

Inside the Wildflower Hotel, Mrs. Finch met Jacob at the desk again.

"Oh, hello, Mr. Payne. Deputy Brady, what are you doing here?"

"Is there any place around here we can talk in private?" Jacob asked.

"Take my study in the back," she said, gesturing them to a small room off the lobby. "Timothy, you know where the cookies are if you boys decide you need some."

Timothy blushed a deep red. "Back here," he mumbled as he led Jacob to the room and closed the door behind them.

Jacob looked around at one of the most opulent rooms he'd encountered since arriving in Arizona. Floral wallpaper, a full bookcase, two finely uphol-stered wingback chairs, and even a marble mantle above the hearth that must have cost a fortune to be shipped all the way out west. No wonder the Finches were treading lightly. Having to leave San Adrian would be disastrous for them.

"How long have you been a deputy?" Jacob began as they settled into the chairs in Mrs. Finch's study. He closed his eyes for a moment to better feel the comfort and luxury all around him. Since he spent most of his days tracking in the untamed wilderness, just a cushion under him when he sat made a world of difference.

"I started about a year ago. A lot of the town don't take me seriously yet. You heard Mrs. Finch offer us cookies." He ducked his head, as though embarrassed. "Right after I turned fourteen, my uncle Alex—he was sheriff, before Horne, see—he deputized me. I was his only one. We don't get much trouble around here. Or when we do, a U.S. Marshal comes. But I moved out here from Philadelphia with my aunt and uncle when I was just a kid, and he kept saying how much he was looking forward to working with me when I was old enough."

"What happened?"

"He died. 'Bout a month ago. The new Sheriff Horne had recently moved to town and was trying to make friends. Or so he said. He and Uncle Alex went out hunting one day and I guess just had some bad luck. Uncle Alex got bit by a rattler, and they were too far from Doctor Pike to save him in time."

"That's a shame, Deputy. I'm real sorry to hear that."

"You can call me Timothy. Everyone else does. I'm mostly sorry for my aunt Maggie. She didn't want to come west and leave her family back in Pennsylvania, but she loved Uncle Alex. And now she's widowed, with no one to take care of her but me."

"I'm sure you do a great job."

He shrugged and blushed again. "I think so. I don't know what we'd do without my deputy pay, though. I'm not a ranch hand or miner or nothin'."

"I don't think you need to worry about that. But, tell me, why did you want to talk to me?"

"I thought maybe the description you gave of that outlaw sounded familiar, but I couldn't remember. Maybe if you gave me more detail it could jog my memory."

Jacob smiled and leaned back in his chair. "You're a good man, Deputy Brady. Timothy. The man we're looking for is short. Dark and graying hair, like I mentioned. Dark eyes. And a deeply scarred face that he tries to hide under a beard."

Timothy paled, his eyes widening like saucers. "What kind of scar?"

Jacob had hoped the boy could make the connection on his own. "It looks like a small knife—or maybe a woman's fingernail—scratched him from his left eyebrow all the way down to his jaw."

"No," Timothy whispered.

"You think you might have an idea?"

"What did you say this fella did?"

"He killed his wife. Strangled her. Then, when her parents came visiting to see where she was, he killed them, too, and left his hometown to come hide in the wide open deserts of Arizona."

"Geez," the boy said, leaning back in his chair.

"You think you know this man, Timothy?"

The boy nodded. "It's Sheriff, ain't it?"

Jacob nodded grimly. "Has to be. No matter what name he calls himself, Sheriff Horne matches the description too perfectly to be anyone else. And he's only heaping on the suspicion by mysteriously losing the wanted poster for Jeremiah Blanchard."

Timothy sat straight. "We have to do something."

Jacob hid a smile at the boy's enthusiasm. "We will. I have some ideas. But I don't know how this town will take it, seein' as how they've got a man like that in charge."

"You should talk to my aunt," Timothy said excitedly, almost bouncing in his chair now. "We've lived here for almost ten years. She knows San Adrian better than anyone. Come home to dinner with me."

———

"Aunt Maggie?" Timothy called as they walked in.

The Winthrops' home was a couple blocks off the main street of San Adrian, a modest, wooden house with just two rooms. The main, front room Jacob found himself in housed the kitchen and table, along with a couple chairs by the wide stone fireplace. A thin bedroll was tucked against the wall by the hearth —probably where Timothy slept.

Out of the bedroom tacked on to the back of the main room came Aunt Maggie, and Jacob was stunned for a moment. This woman didn't look old enough to be Timothy's aunt. She was lovely; she had clear white skin with just a smattering of freckles on her nose, and red-blond hair that shone in the firelight. At the top of her high neckline, she wore a delicate brooch with what looked like a lock of hair.

"Evening, ma'am," Jacob said, removing his hat.

"Aunt Maggie, this is Jacob Payne," Timothy said excitedly. "He's going to help us get Sheriff Horne out of San Adrian."

CHAPTER FIVE

After Timothy told his aunt a bit more about the stranger he had just let into their home, Maggie invited Jacob to stay for dinner. They would need to talk over what they could do to handle the new sheriff without putting themselves or anyone else in the town in danger, and Jacob was grateful for their help and insight. Intelligent conversation and two hot meals in one day? He was beginning to feel spoiled. He wanted to be sure to show her how grateful he was for her hospitality.

When Timothy went out to chop wood and gather more water, Jacob offered his assistance to Maggie.

"Is there anything round here that needs doing? Something your husband would have fixed or built, or a chore that's been waiting for the last month?"

Her eyes filled with tears.

"I'm sorry, ma'am. I didn't mean to—"

"No, no. It's fine. You're right. I'm sure there are

some chores that I've been neglecting. But for now . . ."

She thought for a moment then smiled coyly and, to his surprise, actually laughed.

"What?" asked Jacob, bewildered.

"Well . . . there *is* one thing my husband used to do for me that I could use help with. But"—and here she laughed again, blushing furiously—"you won't like it."

"Whatever you need, Mrs. Winthrop. Just tell me. I aim to make myself useful as long as I'm here."

"Well." She took a deep breath as though steeling herself for something unpleasant. She ducked her chin, looking up at him through long eyelashes. "He used to peel the potatoes."

Jacob had expected something a lot worse. He grinned and nodded. "I can do that. I might not look it, but I have actually peeled potatoes before."

"Would you like an apron?" she offered, teasing him.

He was tempted to accept, just to see if he could make her laugh again, but decided not to. She had only been a widow for a month, and it wouldn't be proper for him to be monopolizing her attention that way.

"No, ma'am. I think I can handle a few potato peels. Can't do me any more harm than riding all morning has."

She laughed again and said, "Thank you for that. I haven't laughed since my husband died."

Jacob grew serious. "I was real sorry to hear about that, Mrs. Winthrop. From what Timothy tells me, it sounds like he was a good, generous man. You should have had a long life together."

Tears welled up in the widow's eyes, but she smiled and dabbed them away before they could fall. "He was . . . he was just that. And he would hate what has become of San Adrian now."

"Don't you worry. We'll fix it. Now, where are those potatoes you need peeled?"

A short time later, after Jacob had peeled all the potatoes, Timothy had finished his chores, and Maggie had finished making dinner, the three sat down to the table together.

"I'll say grace, Aunt Maggie," Timothy volunteered.

Jacob bowed his head with the others. As the boy prayed, Jacob appreciated how both Maggie and Timothy could be grateful for what they had and not bitter about what they had lost. It made him all the more determined to help make it right and put Jeremiah behind bars.

As the three dug into the stew Maggie had made, she commented slyly, "My, what wonderfully peeled potatoes we have here."

Jacob grinned. "My own secret recipe."

"I'm sure. Your mama teach you that? Or your wife?" She looked down into her bowl with this last question.

"I did have a wife, ma'am. But she died in the war. Truth be told, that's also where I learned to peel potatoes."

"Well, then." She smiled at him. "I guess I'll have to thank your sergeant."

Jacob couldn't help but voice a nagging thought he had been having since he'd arrived.

"Pardon me for saying so, Mrs. Winthrop, but I don't see how you're old enough to be this boy's aunt."

Maggie smiled and fixed Jacob with a humorous look. "Well, Mr. Payne, you know a lady never reveals her age."

"Of course— I . . . I'm sorry—" he stammered.

She laughed and quickly reassured him. "Timothy's mother was my sister—my *much older* sister. When she and my brother-in-law died, there was no one else to take him in. Alex and I were not yet engaged, but he could see how badly I wanted to give this boy a home. So we got married right away and adopted the child."

"And now he's lost another parent."

Timothy was eating silently, looking down at his plate. Jacob couldn't imagine how hard this last month had been for the boy. Jacob's own relationship with his father had been strained, but at least he had been around through all of Jacob's childhood.

"How has the last month been for you?" Jacob asked Maggie.

Maggie took a bite of her stew before answering, chewing slowly and considering what to say. Jacob stayed quiet, giving her the time she needed to think about it.

"It's been hard, as you can imagine," she said. "Not just the death, but the everyday as well. We never got my husband's last month's pay." She looked down at her bowl, avoiding Jacob's eyes. "Sheriff Horne confiscated it. Claimed it was evidence."

"Evidence? Of what? What is he investigating?"

She shook her head. "I don't know. He says my Alex died of a snakebite, so I haven't a clue what the pay has to do with that."

"Did the undertaker say it was a snakebite?"

She shook her head. "No. That is, I'm not sure. We never discussed it. I just took Sheriff Horne at his word." She studied Jacob's expression. "You think I should have questioned it?"

"Maybe. Maybe not at that moment, but it might be worth looking into now. If he has your husband's pay to dole out, he might be having an easier time bringing those deputies around to his side. But, on the other hand, if we can find evidence of another murder, it might be possible to get the other deputies out of Sheriff Horne's pocket. The fewer men I have to fight to bring him to justice, the better."

Timothy paled at that. "You think you'll have to fight the other deputies?"

Jacob chewed thoughtfully. "I might. But then, there might be a way I don't have to. If the man would just admit what he and I both know, this could be a lot more simple."

He paused when he saw Maggie reach over to squeeze Timothy's hand. The boy was nervous, that was plain. But whether it was at the thought of fighting the other deputies, of his first real job as a law enforcer, or of something else, Jacob didn't know.

"I'm sorry. We don't have to talk about this at dinner."

At this, Timothy finally looked up. "No. I want to. I want to get this guy out of here, if . . . if he really did murder all those people."

Jacob nodded somberly. "He did."

"Then let's do this."

"We will. But we have to be smart about this. We don't want to start a shootout or put any of the other folks here in danger. A man who feels cornered may lash out, and we already know Jeremiah is capable of murder."

Maggie ventured, "You think we need a way to disarm Sheriff Horne—I mean, Jeremiah Blanchard?"

"Maybe. But more than that, men like him need to feel like they're in power. We need to strip him of whatever power he thinks he has."

"How do we do that?" Timothy asked.

"Leave that to me," Jacob said. "What I need from you is something different."

After helping Maggie wash the dishes and clean up after supper, Jacob left the little family alone for the evening. Both Timothy and Maggie had a part in the plan Jacob had come up with for the next day. He wanted to give them time, not only to rest but also to think about if the task ahead was too big of a risk. He had told them over and over that he could take the man on his own—Jacob was used to confronting dangerous men, and Maggie and Timothy were not, in spite of their connection to the previous sheriff—but they'd insisted on helping.

As he strolled along the boardwalk to the right of the street, back through the dark, quiet town, Jacob pondered what he had learned since arriving in town earlier that day.

Talking to Maggie and Timothy had shown him that not only was Sheriff Horne indeed the man he was after, but it was possible he might have another murder on his conscience as well. It seemed like too much of a coincidence that the previous sheriff died not long after the new man showed up in town.

This was a different kind of bounty than Jacob was used to. Instead of being on the run from the law, the murderer had become the law. Not only would Jacob need to overpower the man somehow, but he would also need to make sure that the rest of San Adrian was on board. Every man, woman, and child in town was upholding the criminal's authority at present. He couldn't afford to capture Sheriff Horne only to be captured himself by the gang of deputies.

After a few blocks, Jacob stopped. He looked around. The town seemed all but deserted. He looked up at the night sky; there seemed to be far more stars out here in Arizona than he remembered from his home back east. Or maybe he had just never taken the time to notice.

Lights shone out of the saloon and hotel windows, but almost no sound made it to the abandoned street where Jacob walked. Most of the homes around the Winthrops' were dark and shuttered.

This, more than anything, told him things were off in San Adrian. The one night he spent in Bennettsville, for example, Jacob was greeted with music, laughter, and friendly hey-theres when he walked through town at this same time of night. Here it was different. The people were hiding.

Just before he reached the main street, only a few blocks away from the Winthrops', Jacob heard steps behind him. He paused, looked back, but didn't see anyone. He decided to move from walking along the boardwalk in front of the buildings to walking in the middle of the dusty street. There would be fewer shadows and fewer corners to hide an attacker.

He continued his stroll, and again he heard footsteps mingled with his own. It wasn't someone running up to meet him, but rather a stalker marking his steps, keeping in time but staying back. Jacob turned to look at who was following him, but saw only shadow against the darkened buildings. Whoever it was didn't want to be seen.

"You know I'm armed," he called into the darkness.

Silence.

"If you have something to say, then say it, 'stead of hiding in the shadows like a thief."

Silence . . . and then, from the darkness, a figure began to emerge.

The silhouette of a tall man wearing a long duster and Stetson. Jacob held his ground while the figure approached. As the mystery man closed the distance, stepping into the light spilling from the nearby hotel, the bright reflection of the man's white beard identified him as Deputy Barnes.

Jacob wondered if the sheriff had sent him to follow, or if the man was acting on his own.

He stopped twenty feet away from Jacob.

"Is there something I can help you with, sir?" Jacob asked in a biting tone. "There must be a reason you're skulking around following me."

"We don't want your kind around here."

"My *kind?*" He laughed. "What, men from Virginia? Best tell the sheriff that, then."

"A bounty hunter's got no place here. If you know what's good for you, you'll leave town. Tonight."

Jacob chuckled. "That's your big scary threat? That I should leave town? Let me tell you, mister. I don't aim to leave without Jeremiah Blanchard in tow. Dead or alive. I wasn't the first to hear about him being seen in San Adrian, and I won't be the last."

"So I should end you right now, then?" the deputy said.

Jacob shrugged. If this man meant to kill him, he'd have been shot in the back before even hearing steps behind him. The deputy may be a bad seed, but he wasn't in the same league as Jeremiah.

"I'm warning you . . ." Barnes said.

Jacob didn't move. He didn't draw his own gun, but he also didn't surrender. He wanted this man to know he could not be intimidated. They were standing in the center of the dark main street of San Adrian. It was only nine o'clock, but there was no one else around, no one to witness this bullying.

"Look, mister. There's something that's been bugging me. I don't know why you've thrown your hat in with this murderer, but if you're not careful you'll end up on a wanted poster yourself. So tell me. What's in it for you?"

Deputy Barnes looked taken aback. "What's in it for me? Other than this deputy badge that gives me leave to do whatever I want?" He laughed a hard, brusque bark.

"Surely not whatever you want," Jacob responded.

"You the type of man who'd murder a woman? Like Jeremiah?"

Still with his gun trained on Jacob, he stalked forward a couple steps. "You don't know what you're talking about."

Jacob stood his ground. "You're fooling yourself, friend. It takes a specific kind of man to murder, and not one you can count on being on your side for long. Jeremiah will use you for what he can and then discard you."

"That's all *you* know."

"Then tell me. Why should I walk away now and leave this town to his mercy?"

"Sheriff Horne is a man who gets things done," Barnes said. "Your showing up in town may have interrupted his plans temporarily, but it just bumped you to the top of his list."

Jacob shook his head, disappointed in the man's answer.

"I'll remember your face, you know," Jacob said. "As long as I'm a bounty hunter, I'll be on the lookout for those blue eyes staring out at me from a wanted bill. Doesn't even matter what name you might be going by, Deputy *Barnes*."

The deputy raised his arm, pointing his gun at Jacob's face. Jacob did not flinch. After a moment, the deputy lowered his arm, quickly firing into the dirt right at Jacob's feet.

"I won't tell you again," the deputy said with an angry growl. "The next time I see you, it had better be the back of you on a horse riding west. If you stay in San Adrian, you'll die. Just like your friend Sheriff Winthrop."

Jacob shook his head and turned his back on the deputy, to finish his walk back to his hotel room. He whistled "Battle Hymn of the Republic" as though he hadn't a care in the world.

CHAPTER SEVEN

The next morning, Jacob woke early, spent some time cleaning his gun, and made his way down to the hotel lobby. He had a few loose ends to tie up in San Adrian today, the first being to ask a favor from Mrs. Finch.

"Good morning, Mr. Payne," she said, greeting him with a smile. He eyed today's hat—a narrow gray thing, with a small veil and purple- and green-dyed feathers sticking almost straight up. "Will you be checking out today?"

"Not just yet, Mrs. Finch. I think my business will wrap up later today, but I'll hold on to the room, just in case."

"All right. Well, then, since you'll be our guest a little bit longer, can I offer you some coffee?"

"Coffee would be great. But there's also one other thing you can do for me, ma'am."

"I'm happy to help if I can."

"It's a small thing, I hope—I don't want to interrupt your day. Do you think you could see your way to coming down to the livery this afternoon? Or, probably better, the *street* in front of the livery? Say around one o'clock?"

Mrs. Finch looked confused as she poured the coffee for him. "You need me at the livery? I don't understand . . . I thought your business was with Sheriff Horne. The livery is at the opposite end of town from the jail."

"I don't want to say too much," Jacob said. "It's better if you don't know what to expect. You'll see why when you get there."

She nodded hesitantly, still puzzled. "If we don't have any guests checking in at that time, I'll be there."

"Thank you, ma'am. And thank you for the coffee. Can I get breakfast at Ed's saloon, too?"

She shook her head. "No. Sometimes Mrs. Baker has bread left over from the night before, but you won't get much more than that till lunch, I'm afraid. My offer to supply you with jerky and biscuits still stands, though."

"Thank you. I'd like that."

When Mrs. Finch left to go prepare Jacob's lunch, he wandered out to the boardwalk in front of the hotel. There were still almost no people out in the street. He needed to do something about that. He stepped back inside.

"Mrs. Finch," he said as she returned. "If you happen to talk to any of your neighbors this morning, could you invite them to the livery as well?"

She frowned, and a hint of fear tugged at her face. "I . . . I don't understand, Mr. Payne. Are you trying to draw a crowd? Is something exciting going to happen?" The way she said the word *exciting* made him believe she meant it as anything but.

"Hopefully," he replied. "You'll see when you get there."

When he left the hotel, Jacob spotted Maggie Winthrop coming out of the telegraph office about a block over on the other side of the street. As she stepped off the wooden walkway, the train of her black dress caught on a loose corner and she stopped, bent down, and freed herself. As she stood back up, Maggie caught his eye, adjusted her bonnet, and smiled shyly, but didn't stop to talk. That was okay with Jacob. After their long conversation last night, he knew she had a full day ahead of her.

He began walking in the other direction, toward the next item on his list to make this plan work, but was stopped in his tracks when he overheard a fight.

"I told you—that was your last chance!" a familiar voice shouted behind him. He turned slowly, moving his hand to unhook his hammer loop.

But Sheriff Horne wasn't shouting at him. The little man was sitting on his horse, glaring down at another man standing before him. It took a second, but Jacob realized this was Ed Baker, and as he watched, the sheriff reached down to slap the older man across the face.

Jacob started walking to the saloonkeeper's side, but before he could reach him, Ed was quickly surrounded by three of the sheriff's deputies. Soon Jacob had lost a clear line of sight to him.

Sheriff Horne stayed on his horse. Jacob realized that was the only way he would even be tall enough to reach Ed. "You think you're above the law, Baker? You think you know better? Better than *me*?"

Jacob reached the cluster in the middle of the street and noticed a crowd gathering to watch. Many of the women held hands over their mouths, shocked at the abuse they were witnessing, their men standing with their arms around them protectively but not doing anything to stop the abuse. Ed was beloved in this town, that much Jacob had gathered; but no one, it seemed, was brave enough to step forward to defend him.

Jacob wouldn't be so cowed.

He pushed one of the deputies out of his way just in time to stop the sheriff from hitting Ed again. "Why don't you get down off that horse if you really want a fight?"

The deputies all pushed and grabbed at Jacob, pulling him away from their boss. It took all three of them to subdue him. Jacob didn't want a fight, so he quit struggling. The deputies didn't let go.

"Stop this! What are you hitting him for?" Jacob demanded.

Jeremiah smiled condescendingly down from his perch atop the stallion. "This is San Adrian business, Mr. Payne. Seeing as you're a stranger to this town, I don't really see any reason to enlighten you."

"Ed," Jacob said in a low voice. "What happened?"

The man's cheek was still bright red where he had been smacked, and he glared at the sheriff. His eyes met Jacob's. He was angry, livid even, but still unwilling to say anything. Jacob could understand that. With his whole livelihood dependent on the goodwill of the town, it wouldn't be in his interest to make this fight worse.

"Sheriff Horne!" a woman's voice called over the crowd.

Jacob turned to see a squat redheaded woman coming from up the street and making her way between the men and women watching the scene.

"Sheriff Horne?" As she jogged toward the crowd, she untied and removed her apron, wrapping her hands in the calico. "What has Ed done? Something upset you, sir? That doesn't sound like my Ed." She reached her husband's side and put her arm around his shoulders. Mrs. Baker was a full head shorter than her husband, but she still managed to look like a protective mother hen. She used the apron in her hand to clean the dirt off Ed's hands and face from where he fell in the street.

"Well, ma'am," the sheriff said plaintively, "your husband has some outlandish ideas. Seems he thinks that *he's* the one gets to decide how things are 'round here. But maybe you're right—maybe it's not like him. Might be he picked up some things when talking to some of the more unsavory characters 'round here."

He looked pointedly at Jacob. Mrs. Baker followed his gaze and hardened her expression against the bounty hunter.

"You might be right, Sheriff Horne," she said. "We'll be sure to be more careful about who we serve from now on."

Without saying good-bye or asking the sheriff's leave, Ed and his wife cut through the crowd and back toward their saloon. Jacob was still being restrained by two of the deputies, but when he tried to shake them loose, they relaxed their grip.

"Beating an unarmed man, Sheriff? Is that the way to win hearts and minds around here?"

Jacob spat at the foot of the horse Jeremiah sat on and turned to go. As he passed, he noticed a look of concern cross Deputy Conroy's face. Jacob noted how the big man stepped back from the sheriff and thought maybe he was already making inroads.

CHAPTER EIGHT

As Jacob walked away from Sheriff Horne and his deputies in the middle of the street, he had to weave his way through the crowd that had gathered to watch the commotion. Many of the people he passed looked at him curiously, some not so friendly. Some of them were beginning to murmur to one another, and he caught snatches of conversation as he moved through the group.

"He shouldn't—"

"What could have—"

"I don't like this."

It was starting.

Jacob hoped that once the townspeople began to realize they could fight back against Sheriff Horne's dictatorship, the tide would turn. If even Deputy Conroy was beginning to change his opinion, like Jacob suspected, this might all work out without any more bloodshed. As long as the sheriff had the town's tacit support, the man could do whatever he wanted; but it looked as if that was beginning to change.

The scene Jacob was now leaving could have been the perfect opportunity to take down the sheriff—but it was too fast. Too soon. He hadn't had the proper time to collect all the pieces he needed. He'd just have to try again.

The day was beginning to warm as he walked away from the crowd, reading the signs above each storefront. He pulled out the biscuits and jerky Mrs. Finch had given him and gnawed while he looked. Jacob had one last piece of the puzzle to fit in before making a new attempt to subdue and capture the outlaw. He had a nagging suspicion, and only one person could help alleviate it.

He found the undertaker's office a block away from the jail. The sign above the door read Charles & Son Undertakers, and when Jacob walked in he found the older Mr. Charles working bent over his desk.

"Pardon me. I'm sorry to bother you, sir," Jacob said, taking his hat in hand.

"Nonsense. Come in, come in," the older man said, standing to greet Jacob. He was slightly hunched over, as though the weight of all the deaths he had overseen remained on his shoulders. His white mustache was neatly trimmed and his spectacles clean and clear. "I'm Eugene Charles. What can I do for you, young man? Can I offer you coffee?" He looked toward the doorway behind Jacob. "You don't seem to have a body in tow."

"No, sir. Not yet, at least."

"Not yet?" Mr. Charles frowned. "Death is nothing

to be flippant about, young man. But I'm forgetting myself—I don't believe we've met. You're new to San Adrian, are you not?"

"I am, Mr. Charles. Just here for a couple days, God willing. And I'm sorry—I don't mean to be flippant. I was wondering if I could ask you something."

He narrowed his eyes suspiciously. "What did you say your name was?"

"Payne. Jacob Payne." He sat in the wooden chair across the desk from Eugene and placed his hat on his knee.

"Ah, yes," the older man said, relaxing back into his chair. "I've heard of you."

This surprised Jacob. "You have?"

"Oh, yes. Ed Baker is one of my good friends, and we talked just last night. He told me you were looking for Sheriff Horne, so I thought it'd only be a matter of time before you ended up in my office."

"Oh?"

"Glad to see you're here alive, if I could speak honestly. I thought it might be possible you'd get here on a slab instead, the way you're going after the sheriff."

"Well, to be honest, sir, I still might. Again, not to be flippant about death. But Sheriff Horne is a dangerous character, and I seem to be making him mad."

He chuckled. "I bet you are."

"In fact, if I might be so bold, sir . . . you might think about looking in on your friend Mr. Baker later today. I just witnessed him being beaten and upbraided in the middle of the street by Sheriff Horne himself."

Mr. Charles frowned. "Right in the street, you say? Well. That's no way to treat a grown man, let alone a prominent citizen of the town the sheriff has sworn to protect. I'll talk to Ed about it. You said you wanted to ask me something?"

"Yes, sir. I was wondering if I could trouble you about something that's been bothering me. I understand you might not want to get involved, so I can do my best to leave your name out of it."

Eugene smiled grimly. "Just be out with it, young man."

"Well, Deputy Brady and Mrs. Winthrop told me about how Sheriff Winthrop died. I was wondering if you had seen the body, and if you could confirm it was a snakebite that killed him."

Eugene looked at Jacob, rubbing his chin thoughtfully. "What makes you ask that?"

"Just a hunch. Seems like quite a coincidence if it happened the way Horne is telling it. I would think a man like Winthrop, a man who's lived out here in the desert for years, would have more caution and know how to avoid the snakes."

Eugene nodded. "That's true. Well, Mr. Payne, I can tell you this much."

Jacob sat forward, leaning on his elbows.

"Sheriff Winthrop did indeed suffer a snakebite. Based on my examination, it did seem to be from a rattler, but I can't be completely positive."

"All right, then. Thank you—"

"But that's not all."

Jacob abruptly shut his mouth to listen.

"The snakebite appeared to have happened after the man was already dead."

"What?" It felt as if a stone had dropped into the pit of Jacob's stomach. This was as bad as he suspected. "How can you be sure?"

"There was no blood around the bite wound. The poor man had likely already bled out from a bullet to the gut."

"A bullet to the gut? That's a lot of blood . . . how is it no one else saw the gut wound?"

"Hard to say, but I would guess that Horne—excuse me, *Sheriff* Horne—put Sheriff Winthrop's vest and jacket back on the corpse after the wound occurred."

"That's despicable."

Mr. Charles nodded. "How he managed that, I can't say. We can't be sure about the sequence of events unless Sheriff Horne tells us himself. Putting the clothes back on after the fact would have hid the blood from anyone giving the body a cursory look and would not have been discovered until my son took over management of the corpse."

Jacob leaned back in his chair, shaking his head. Just hearing about a man using the law as a cover to get away with murder made him incredibly angry. Angry as a man who was loyal to the law. Angry on behalf of Maggie and Timothy and what they had lost. Angry on behalf of all the citizens of San Adrian, like Ed Baker.

"Did you tell anyone else what you found?"

Eugene shook his head. "My son knows, of course,

but he's discreet. Who would I tell? The new sheriff or one of his thugs? No, I kept that information to myself. Winthrop was already dead, and I thought it best to not make waves with the new man in charge."

"If I am able to capture Sheriff Winthrop and bring him to justice, would you be willing to testify against him?"

"If he's captured? If he's brought to trial, then yes. I will tell all that I know. But as long as he is running this town, I trust you'll keep this information to yourself."

"Why tell me, if I may ask? You're not worried about me revealing it?"

"The way I see it, Mr. Payne, if you're going after this man, you are at even bigger risk than I am. It can't possibly do you any good to reveal this information unless you're absolutely sure it will be to your success."

Jacob nodded and stood to say good-bye. "Very true, Mr. Charles. I take it you've worked with a lot of lawmen in your life."

The older man smiled. "They come and go, and yet I'm still here. Good luck to you, young man."

With that confirmed, Jacob knew it was time. He had all the pieces he needed lined up to kill or capture Jeremiah Blanchard.

CHAPTER NINE

When he left the undertaker's, it was almost one o'clock. The morning had gone by quickly, but he had to trust that enough time had passed for what Jacob was planning. He had an appointment—the last domino that needed to fall before he could capture Jeremiah without difficulty from the rest of the town. It would be a risk, but it was the only way Jacob knew to get close to the sheriff; otherwise, there would always be a deputy in the way.

The undertaker's office was near the jail, but Jacob walked right past it without even a glance. He was looking for another target—the stretch of main street out front of the livery. It would be almost as far away as he could get from the jail and still be in San Adrian.

As he approached, he counted four or five people standing outside the door, including Sheriff Horne's loyal deputies. Jacob scanned the crowd quickly, grateful that Maggie wasn't there to see what was about to happen. She knew about this step; perhaps she was avoiding the scene on purpose. That was just fine, Jacob thought.

As Jacob closed the final yards before the crowd, he steeled himself. What he was about to do would not be pleasant, but it would be necessary. A common trait of the job.

"You," he bellowed. "You think you can spread stories about me and I won't find out?"

The waiting crowd all turned to see who was yelling. Most of them backed up when they saw Jacob bearing down on them with all his six-plus feet of muscle. Only Deputy Brady held his ground, defiantly raising his chin and answering in the affirmative—just as they'd practiced.

"You're the one telling tales on me?"

"That's right, Payne. I— I did," Timothy said as he stood up straighter and squared his shoulders. "What are you going to do about it?"

He must have dug deep for his bravado. Anyone could see Jacob was at least twice his body weight, nearly all of it in muscle. The bounty hunter loomed over the kid. He kept his hands off his gun but took his coat off and threw it in the dust to give himself greater range of movement. He rolled his sleeves up as Timothy backed up a couple steps.

Jacob shoved Timothy off the boardwalk and into the dusty street. The kid stumbled, backing up several long steps into the road. A man riding past had to swerve his horse out of the way, and shouted at Timothy as he did.

Jacob jumped down off of the wooden planks to go after Timothy, the dust creating clouds around his feet. "Deputy Brady," he said. "Only a coward would run now."

His voice was cold, but he tried to communicate something different to Timothy with his eyes. Jacob realized they should have discussed this part of the plan in a little more detail before now.

"Hey!" one of the deputies yelled.

Jacob shot him a look of loathing, wordlessly daring him to interrupt. He did not.

Timothy recovered his balance. "Stay out of this, Deputy Conroy, Deputy Nelson," he called to the crowd still standing around the livery. "This is between me and Payne."

Jacob had reached the kid and used both his wide palms to shove him in the chest, knocking him to the ground. Timothy landed hard on his rear, accidentally putting his hand in a stinking pile of manure that had been dropped not long ago. The look of disgust on the deputy's face came and went in a flash. He didn't dwell. He shook it off and wiped his hand on his pants.

Jacob wrinkled his nose reflectively. That smell . . . he'd need to be even more diligent about not letting the kid hit him.

Timothy scrambled to his feet and held up his fists in front of him, as though he had the slightest idea how to fight. He bounced on the balls of his feet, ready to dart to the right or left depending on how Jacob came at him.

"Goodness, someone stop them!" a woman cried.

Jacob didn't bother to see who. The more people that gathered, the better. The more citizens the woman called to the scene to witness what should be about to happen, the more smoothly Jacob's plan would work.

The look of fear on Timothy's face almost made Jacob hesitate, but he knew better. This was what had to happen. Timothy was as good as a grown man now, and a deputy of the law would know he was at risk for this. This was what he wanted, too; Jacob had given him plenty of opportunity to back out.

Jacob reeled back and swung, punching Timothy in the jaw and knocking him to the dirt.

"Oh my!" Mrs. Finch exclaimed.

Timothy climbed to his feet and rushed Jacob, putting his shoulder down and running hard at him. When the kid made contact, Jacob had to back up a few steps but managed to hold his ground. He wrapped his arms around the kid and tossed him a few feet away from him.

"You think you can just throw me around?" Timothy cried at him as he regained his balance, his voice cracking. "I'm a deputy! You can't put your hands on me. Wait till I tell Sheriff Horne."

Jacob punched Timothy in the nose, wincing at the crack he both felt and heard. Timothy stumbled backward a few paces before losing his footing and landing in the dirt yet again. Blood bloomed from the boy's nostrils, dripping down over his mouth. He spat a bloody mist to the ground near Jacob's feet. The boy had yet to knock the bounty hunter down, and Jacob almost felt bad.

"You do that. You call Sheriff Horne. That's

exactly the man I want to see. He should be here protecting his deputy, but where is he? The coward."

Timothy's eyes grew wide at Jacob's declaration. "I don't— I think maybe—"

"Call him," Jacob continued, turning to the crowd to address them as well. "We already know Horne isn't man enough to keep control of this town without resorting to violence. We all saw him attacking an unarmed man earlier."

"Jacob," Timothy said softly.

"Stop right there," a voice said behind the bounty hunter.

But Jacob didn't stop. He pulled Timothy to his feet, only so he could punch him to the ground again.

"Stop, I say. You are assaulting an officer of the law!" The voice was closer now, but still Jacob didn't stop.

A crack rang out, crashing through Jacob's focus and interrupting his attack. After half a second, he realized his left arm hurt. No, it *burned*. And when he paused in his punching to reach up and touch the spot, his fingers came away wet and red.

He had been shot.

His plan may be unraveling.

CHAPTER TEN

Jacob was still looking at the blood on his fingers when he heard, "Jacob Payne, you are under arrest for assaulting an officer."

Deputy Timothy Brady lay in the dirt at Jacob's feet, wincing as he felt his jaw and checked to make sure all his teeth were still in his head. His nose had bled a bit, staining the front of his shirt, and was quickly swelling up. Jacob hoped he hadn't hurt him too bad. The kid had a manic gleam of triumph in his eyes—even through the injury, he was enjoying himself.

The gunfire had paused the fight. In the lull, the other three deputies rushed to seize Jacob and stop him from attacking Timothy further. Two grabbed each of his massive arms, while the third stabbed him in the back with the barrel of his revolver.

A crowd was fully gathered now. Jacob noticed Mrs. Finch's hat standing tall like the mast of a ship above the heads of the others, the green and purple feathers glinting in the sun. She had come just as he'd asked her to. He hoped she would be quick enough to understand why. Their shouting and carrying on had drawn many of the other citizens of San Adrian to the crowd as well.

But, as he looked around at the crowd surrounding them, he cringed. Jacob had not intended to get shot. His carefully crafted plan was showing cracks. The whole left side of his body felt heavy as the blood drained from his arm. He made a brief attempt to shake the deputies off, but he didn't have the strength to fight back against three grown men holding him immobilized.

None of the crowd came to defend him. And why would they? They hadn't done anything earlier, when the sheriff was beating Ed Baker for no good reason. Why would they lift a finger in protest now, when this stranger had clearly provoked his own attack?

"You have no authority to arrest me," Jacob said through clenched teeth.

From behind him Deputy Nelson said, "You shut up, Payne. You were caught attacking a deputy. You can't get away with that."

"Where's Blanchard?"

"Who?"

"Your boss. He told you he's Sheriff Horne, but he's a murderer by any name. Jeremiah Blanchard."

"You shut up," Deputy Conroy said, punching Jacob in the mouth.

Shot, restrained, and now punched, Jacob was feeling his prey slip through his fingers. "Where is he?" he yelled.

The deputy punched him again, and Jacob felt his teeth smash against his lower lip. He spat out a mouthful of blood at the feet of his assaulter.

"Bring him here."

Jacob tried to glance behind him, where Jeremiah Blanchard stood in the middle of the street, forcing the few riders to either go around him or stop altogether. Jacob had wanted a crowd, and now his target was helping him create one.

Jeremiah waited about twenty feet away, looking gleeful to finally have a reason to attack Jacob. The deputies marched Jacob over to their boss and one of the deputies kicked the back of Jacob's knee, forcing him to the ground. He stifled a groan as his arm was wrenched at an unnatural angle, the muscle's movement pushing the bullet deeper inside.

"Jacob Payne," the man said, smiling. "You are under arrest. What a shame to have such a promising career cut short."

"You have no authority to arrest me," Jacob said. "You're no sheriff. You're not even named John Horne. You're a fraud." He spat blood again, this time on Jeremiah's feet.

The outlaw jumped back, but blood still speckled the bottom of his pant legs. When he stepped forward again, he launched a kick into Jacob's ribs.

"Ah, you see, though, I have the power," he said as Jacob groaned in pain. "I have the deputies. I have the weapon. I am the sheriff of San Adrian, and I am declaring you guilty of assaulting a deputy."

"Fine," Jacob said, seeing his chance. "Let's

pretend you can arrest me. Take me to a judge, and we'll see who is in custody then."

"Oh, Mr. Payne, perhaps you misheard me. I said that *I* find you guilty of the charge. Now to just decide on your sentence."

"Wait—" Timothy started.

"You're not the law," Jacob said, cutting the boy off. "You need a judge. You don't get to decide guilt."

"No, I think you're guilty," Jeremiah said. "In fact, I'm sure of it. There's no need to bother taking you all the way to a judge in Tucson."

"You are not the law," Jacob said again, raising his voice for all to hear.

"I am now. I am the law, and I sentence you to death."

"What? No!" Timothy yelled.

Jacob struggled against his captors, but his injured arm put him at a disadvantage. He couldn't overpower three deputies with only one good arm, even if he was on his feet.

"Let go of me!" he cried. "You can't think this is right."

Deputy Nelson looked uncomfortable, but he didn't abandon his post. The other deputies held him fast. Jacob caught Maggie's eye across the crowd; her anguished expression made him wish he could shield her from this.

"No man is judge, jury, and executioner," Jacob shouted to the crowd.

He heard murmurs of confusion and protest all around, but it didn't seem as though any of them would be brave enough to stop the man. Jeremiah crossed the final steps to where Jacob was held kneeling on the ground.

Jacob took a deep breath and closed his eyes. He had done all he could to expose this alleged sheriff as the murderer he was. Just as Jacob felt the cold iron against his forehead, he heard the sound of several horses galloping up the street.

CHAPTER ELEVEN

With a gun pointed at his head, Jacob didn't dare turn to look to see who rode up the street, but he counted the hooves of three horses. The crowd that had gathered to watch the altercation began whispering and murmuring in confusion.

"Drop your weapon," Jacob heard a familiar voice say. "Step away from that man."

Instead of stepping away from him, Jeremiah grabbed Jacob's injured arm and yanked him to his feet. This was the first time the two men were so close together, and Jacob realized the outlaw only came up to his broad shoulders. The barrel of the gun was soon jammed hard into his ribs, still bruised from Blanchard's kick. Jacob could feel the bruising deepen, but he stayed quiet, watching the riders arrive.

At the end of the street from the south side of town, and coming closer with every second, was

Sheriff Williams of Bennettsville and two of his deputies.

"I said drop your weapon!" Sheriff Williams yelled. "Give up, Blanchard. Your reign is over."

Without dismounting, Sheriff Williams held up the wanted poster Jacob had last seen the morning before. Even from this distance, it was easy to identify Jeremiah Blanchard's scowling face.

"What are you doing here?" Jeremiah said to the sheriff of Bennettsville with a threatening growl.

"Upholding the law. One of these fine citizens of San Adrian telegraphed me to come identify you. You're not fooling anyone. Now come quietly so no one else gets hurt."

"The hell I will," Jeremiah said. "My deputies will arrest you for attempting to assault an officer of the law. Who says I'm the man in that poster?"

"*I* say," Jacob retorted. He was rewarded with a punch to the gut from Deputy Barnes.

"*I* say," Sheriff Williams echoed from on top of his horse.

"*I* say," Timothy said defiantly, making sure to stay close to Sheriff Williams and out of reach of any of the other San Adrian deputies. He raised his gun and pointed it at Jeremiah.

"You better watch yourself, kid," Jeremiah said.

Deputies Nelson and Conroy looked less and less sure, as the crowd around them grew more hostile, calling for this fight to end.

"Here. See for yourself." Sheriff Williams thrust the paper at the man nearest him, Deputy Conroy.

The deputy quickly scanned over the document.

He shook his head. "The description matches. That's definitely him, even with this beard trying to cover his scar."

"You trying to hide your identity with that new scruff, Blanchard?" Jacob demanded. He felt the gun barrel dig deeper into his ribs.

"You murdered your wife?" Deputy Conroy said. "That's—" He shook his head, speechless.

Jeremiah removed his gun from Jacob's side and pointed it now at Deputy Conroy. "You got something to say? Huh? You want to try to take me on now that you know what I'm capable of?"

In the commotion, Jacob backed away, out of arm's reach from Jeremiah, and unfastened his hammer loop. He thought quickly. He could easily outdraw Jeremiah, but any bullets shot with this many people around ran the risk of injuring more than just their target. He didn't want to get shot, but more than that, he didn't trust the other man's aim.

Deputy Conroy thrust the wanted poster at Deputy Nelson. "Here. Read it."

Nelson scanned it quickly, spitting when he reached the end. "Woman killer," he hurled at Jeremiah.

"Murderer!" called a voice from the crowd.

Jeremiah turned from deputy to deputy, waving his gun around wildly. "I am the sheriff of this town!" he shouted. "You all need to *respect* me!" He fired his gun into the air.

That decided it for Jacob. He quickly drew his revolver, pulled the hammer back, aimed, and squeezed the trigger, landing his shot exactly in Jeremiah's right calf.

"Argh!" the outlaw cried, collapsing.

He was injured enough to keep him from running, as Jacob intended—but not enough to keep him from shooting. His aim was too wild to try to disarm him just yet.

"I am the sheriff!" he shouted again, though it was somewhat distorted by his moan of pain.

"Not any more," Jacob said. "There is no Sheriff Horne. There never was."

"You thought you'd get away with changing your name just because you had destroyed the wanted bill?" Timothy said. He was still holding his jaw from where Jacob had punched him, but his anger shone through in spite of whatever pain he might still be in.

"You destroyed the wanted poster, too?" Deputy Conroy said, marveling. "That is low. That's not upholding the law. Where is your respect for your duty?" He took a deep breath and deliberately turned his gun to point at Jeremiah.

The outlaw cursed, but still would not surrender. He fired again toward Sheriff Williams, but it went high and wide.

"Sheriff Williams," Jacob said, offering his last nail in the coffin. "When you take this man before the judge, be sure you let him know Blanchard is under suspicion for murdering at least one more man. Sheriff Winthrop died while alone in the desert with Blanchard. I don't think that's a coincidence. Mr. Charles, the undertaker of this town, has agreed to testify about what he witnessed when the body came in."

"Sheriff Winthrop, too?" Deputy Nelson shook his head, relaxing his gun arm and looking dejected for just a short moment. He stopped himself, looking up again and glaring at Jeremiah. He took a deep breath and in one quick step moved from pointing his gun at Jacob, to pointing it at Jeremiah, now joining his fellow deputies.

The outlaw let out a frustrated hiss. "You'll regret that."

"You get one last chance, Blanchard. Surrender. You no longer have even a single deputy on your side," Jacob said.

Jeremiah growled, glaring at Jacob. He looked around, realizing how many guns were pointed at him. Even Ed Baker had a Winchester in his arms, trained at the man. The tide had turned. Deputy Barnes had left his side, and was now standing closer to Jacob, with his gun holstered, arms harmlessly at his side.

Seeing his last ally had deserted him, Jeremiah cursed, tossed his gun to the ground, and surrendered.

CHAPTER TWELVE

While many guns were still pointed at the outlaw, the Bennettsville deputies dismounted and bound him, wrists and ankles together. As soon as it was clear that Jeremiah Blanchard had been contained, Jacob finally let himself relax. He had done his job; the town was safe again.

The moment he felt himself let his guard down, Jacob spotted Maggie Winthrop's gleaming hair pushing through the crowd. Her expression was frantic as she checked on Timothy. Once she had ascertained that he was fine, she turned to Jacob.

"Let me clean you up," Maggie said. She took his uninjured arm and led Jacob to the boardwalk on the side of the street, guiding him to sit down. The sleeve was torn and bloody where the bullet had gone in. "I'm going to have to tear your shirt, Mr. Payne."

"That's all right. With the reward from catching Blanchard I can get a new shirt," he said with a smile.

She handed him a small bottle of whiskey. He took

only a mouthful while she washed and disinfected his wound.

"This is going to hurt," she said softly.

He nodded. "Go ahead." He had been shot before. He'd had bullets extracted before. He knew what to expect, but that wouldn't make it hurt any less. He balled up his fist as she carefully, delicately pulled the bullet out of his bicep with a pair of tongs. He didn't move, he didn't squirm, he didn't cry out, and she was done in no time.

"Now, you really should rest a bit," Maggie said, fixing his bandage over the wound. "I don't want to hear about you getting in any fights or inspiring any shootouts for at least a couple hours."

Jacob laughed. "A couple hours? No promises, but I think I can handle that."

"If you come to supper at our home tonight, that should keep you busy for at least a little while. You won't be able to peel potatoes, though."

"Then I guess we won't be eating potatoes," he said with a laugh.

She smiled but then grew serious, bending her face closer to his. "Jacob," she began in a quiet voice. "That is, Mr. Payne. I need to thank you for what you did for us. For me. I never thought I would see justice for my Alex, and then you come to town and not only uncover the truth of his death but also rid our town of his murderer."

"It's my job, ma'am. I'm happy to do it." He wanted to put his arm around her, to squeeze her hand, to comfort her in some way, but he knew he had done all he could. "I'm just glad you weren't around to see the part of my job where I had to rough up your nephew."

She smiled. "I stayed away from that as much as I could. Knowing it had to happen was one thing. Seeing it happen would have been quite another. Although, that reminds me . . . maybe I'll set you to cleaning bloodstains out of Timothy's shirt when you come over later."

Jacob grinned. "Whatever I can do to pull my weight."

"Oh, Mr. Payne!" Mrs. Finch exclaimed as she burst through the crowd. "Mr. Payne, that was so brave of you. I knew, *we* knew, there was something not right about Sheriff Horne, but I never would have dreamed he was such a horrible character."

A round man, shorter than her, stood just behind Mrs. Finch, his hands stuffed in his pockets as he let her lead the way.

Jacob stood to greet them, keeping his left arm resting at his side. "This must be Mr. Finch."

"Norman Finch, at your service. We've upgraded your room at the Wildflower Hotel. We're hoping you'll still stay the night with us before moving on again."

"You didn't have to do that."

"Oh, Mr. Payne, you must stay," Mrs. Finch gushed. "And come to supper at our home. Give me your laundry to do before you leave. There must be something more we can do for you."

"That's very kind of you, ma'am. I've already made plans for supper, but I'm much obliged for the room."

"Mr. Payne, can I speak to you?" Sheriff Williams said, interrupting the women's fawning.

The sheriff led the way to the San Adrian jail and let himself in.

Jacob again found himself watching out the window of a jail while the sheriff escorted one of his captures. This time, though, instead of taking the thief to a cell in this jail, Jacob watched the Bennettsville deputy ride off to their own jail with Jeremiah Blanchard in tow. He was lashed to a horse, and none too gently.

When he returned from giving his deputy instructions, Sheriff Williams lowered his giant frame into the chair behind the desk of the San Adrian jail. "Can't say this fits me any better than the chair at home." He dug through the mess of paperwork on the desk to find a pencil and scrap of paper to make a note. "Well, Payne, that's a second reward for you in just as many days. Since we don't have the cash on hand, where do you want this one sent?"

"Wire it to Mrs. Maggie Winthrop in San Adrian."

"All of it, Payne? What are you hunting bounties for if you're just going to give all the money to someone else?"

"This man murdered her husband, and she was just as useful in getting him caught as I was. She deserves the reward and she can use the help. This will keep her from having to worry about money for a while."

"Want me to send a telegram along with it?"

"No. She doesn't need to know who it's from."

"She'll know."

Jacob smiled. "She might guess, but I'll never say—and you'd better not either."

"You're a good man, Payne. As long as you swear to me you won't go hungry by giving up this money, I'm happy to pass it along to the sheriff's widow."

"Thanks, Sheriff."

"You know where you're off to next? San Adrian might like to see you stand for Sheriff now that Horne—I mean Jeremiah—is gone."

"No. Thank you. I'm not meant to be stuck in one spot very long. There will be another criminal that crosses my path sooner if I move on to the next town. I'll stay here another night, enjoy another supper with Mrs. Winthrop and give the Finches my business, but I'll be on my way in the morning. Thank you all the same."

"Well, in that case, how about that drink I promised you before you head to supper?" Sheriff Williams asked.

"I'll take you up on that. I bet Ed would be happy to see us," Jacob responded with a smile.

DANGER IN THE CANYON

CHAPTER ONE

Jacob Payne dismounted. The scorching Arizona sun beat relentlessly down, drenching his dark, close-cropped hair with sweat and plastering it to his skull. With one hand he took off his hat to fan his face, and with the other took hold of the reins to lead his pinto down through the uneven, rocky bank of the dry riverbed. The sandy ground shifted and crumbled under his feet.

As he took the first step through the brush, the dirt bank collapsed and one of the ragweed plants uprooted altogether. Jacob almost lost his balance as he slipped down the low slope. Even a desert plant couldn't hang on forever without water, and Jacob knew he would be the same way. A body could only take so much.

The tall man paused to let the dirt and rocks tumble down the rest of the bank while he replaced his hat. His shirt clung to his sides, tight across his broad shoulders, the sweat running down his back under the layers. He blinked back the sweat dripping into his eyes. Once the rocks had settled he would lead his horse across, searching again for both water and his man. He couldn't risk his horse making a false step. He couldn't risk sweating out all his water. He still had a ways to go.

The bounty hunter had been on the outlaw's trail for three days now, winding away from Tucson, far to the south and the west, following his mark. While he thought he had packed enough water when he set out, the canteen was already running dangerously low. He had been able to supplement a little along the way, but if he didn't find a substantial source of water soon he might have to give up this hunt.

Jacob had never walked away from a reward once he began tracking, and he had no intention of starting now. The man he was after would need water just as badly, and Jacob knew he could best him.

Jacob led the pinto down the final few crumbling steps to the riverbed. Sparse, hardy desert weeds and animal burrows were beginning to crop up in the middle of the dry plane, life continuing in the absence of running water. After a few feet, the dry, cracked dirt revealed the faint impression of a pair of horse-shoes. Jacob squatted down and compared them to the depth of his own print. Judging from how much dust had been blown away, he guessed he was standing right where Jed Corker had crossed less than one day past.

He stood again, looking for further prints, eyeing the horizon, and considering his options. Jacob paused to swallow a mouthful of water from his canteen.

Before he'd left town, several long-time locals had warned Jacob about the monsoon they expected any day, pressing him to take an extra coil of rope and more jerky than he had packed. "You'll not be able to see your own hand," they had said. "You've not seen a storm of this like." He had not yet been in such a squall here in Arizona, but he'd heard tell of torrential storms that could appear as though out of nowhere, dumping gallons of water in only an hour, or of a wall of dust sweeping across the territory, obscuring every living thing in its path.

But Jacob had been in storms before; this didn't concern him none. He packed his saddlebags, filled his canteen, and didn't fret. When he had left Virginia almost a year ago to come west, he'd thought he was escaping the wet and the humidity. The fierce heat of the Arizona desert was like a balm, and for the last few months he felt like he was truly dry for the first time in his life.

Such scorching drought, he knew, would only be bearable for as long as he had water to drink. He'd gotten used to recognizing signs that he needed more water, since he'd taken to spending so much time in the desert. A monsoon would give him all the water he could want, but he couldn't count on that storm finding him. He had been rationing as well as he could, but Jacob would need to find other sources if he was going to make his way back.

Standing in the middle of the riverbed, Jacob scanned the horizon ahead of him. In this midday heat, most of the desert animals would be resting deep underground. Without a lick of wind to stir the shrubs, Jacob heard only his own breathing. Wherever Corker had got to, he was not within hearing distance.

About a mile or two on up, small hills rose and so did Jacob's hopes. He squinted his eyes against the sun and made out some low mesquite trees and what looked like a canyon extending between the hills. From this distance, it was impossible to tell how wide or deep the canyon was, but there was an unmistakable shady area beckoning to him. He'd have to keep an eye out for prints, but a cool hole like that would be where Corker would head to. Shade, maybe even water. Trees meant there must be some kind of dampness, at least.

Jacob grinned to himself. Unless he was much mistaken about the other man's desire for survival, he expected to find his target and make his arrest that afternoon—maybe even within the hour.

"Well, Paint," Jacob said as he poured water into the palm of his wide hand and offered it to the horse. "What do you think? Seems Corker is probably up there waiting for us, huh? Ready to keep going?"

The horse lapped up the water eagerly and nuzzled Jacob's ear. The bounty hunter nodded, took hold of the reins, and continued leading his companion through the arid terrain.

Three days earlier, before setting off into the desert, Jacob had been eating supper at San Xavier Cafe in Tucson, his favorite meal when in town. The locals were friendly, and Bonnie, who brought meals most nights, always had a coy smile for him. He had helped some of her unwanted suitors find the door more than once, and she had yet to stop thanking him.

By the front door, Bobby played a lively tune on the piano, humming under his breath while the cafe filled with regulars. Edwin Hogg caught Jacob's eye with a grin as he crossed the threshold. He'd be wantin' a hand or three of poker, no doubt, Jacob thought. He took another bite. Jackrabbit stew and coffee filled Jacob's stomach while he contemplated his next move.

The U.S. Marshal's office down the street had a stack of wanted posters nearly two feet high, and all Jacob had to do was pick one. The number of degenerate men pouring west into Arizona meant Jacob would be kept busy. Men who had not been able to find their place after the war ended. Men who already had murders or thefts on their conscience and came out to the open desert where they thought they could get away with more. Jacob had come to the cafe for supper, yes, but also for information. If anyone in town had even a hint of where one of these outlaws was at, Jacob would follow the trail without a second thought.

Jacob had just asked Bonnie for a second cup of coffee and more cornbread when one of the town's deputies burst through the door, yanked his hat from his head, and pitched it across the room at an empty table.

"Blast!" Deputy Lowry exclaimed, stomping after his hat.

He followed that outburst by kicking over the closest empty chair, causing the two women seated at that table to gasp in surprise.

The deputy stomped off after his hat, sinking down into the chair at the table in the corner, alone, and crossing his arms across his chest, chewing furiously.

"What seems to be the problem, deputy?" Jacob asked after him. "Somethin' happen?"

He stood to right the chair and apologize to the poor surprised women. They both held hands over their chests as though trying to still their beating hearts, looking askance at the fuming deputy.

"Damn straight, somethin' happened!" He turned his head and spat a straight stream of tobacco juice into the spittoon by the wall behind him. "Jed Corker escaped."

Jacob took his now-full cup of coffee from his original seat and sat down across from Deputy Lowry in his corner table. "Corker? Ain't he with the Slippery Stone Gang?"

"He is. Or was. It's none too clear. He held up the Valleseco Bank on his own, with no help from Stone or anyone else in the gang. Just a couple days ago, this was. Managed to kill two tellers who didn't move fast enough for his liking and wound a woman, one of the bank's customers. Violence ain't Stone's way. I don't know that he's ever killed an innocent. My guess is Corker's out on his ear and desperate to make do."

"But you caught him, didn't ya?"

"We did. Deputy Little'n me caught up with him not far outside of town and was bringing him back to stand trial when he slipped away from us."

"How'd that happen?"

"No tellin'. Elliott 'Slippery' Stone must've taught him a trick or two. Woke up this morning and he was gone. Stole a horse, but he left his take from Valleseco Bank. Me'n Deputy Little raced back here to send the telegrams out to nearby towns. Wayne City and Solano both have banks less than a day's ride from here. If Corker's feelin' desperate, he might try again."

Jacob nodded darkly. "There's nothing more vicious than a desperate man."

Lowry spat again. "I don't like it one bit."

Jacob stood up.

"Tell me exactly where you lost him. I can pick up the trail."

Deputy Lowry remained in his seat and leaned back to put his boots on the table. A fine layer of dust shook loose and coated the wooden surface. "Now, look, Payne. Corker is a dangerous creature, and the Valleseco bank ain't offered a bounty of any kind. I don't want you to go gettin' yourself killed for nothing."

Jacob took one last swig of the bitter black coffee before setting the mug down on the table. The heat and the adrenaline of the hunt coursed through his limbs. Edwin and his card game could wait.

"Beggin' your pardon, deputy, but the man killed two people, wounded more, and could be on his way to do more damage. If I can stop him, I will. Reward or no reward. Tell me where you lost him."

Once he had wrung all the details he could from Deputy Lowry, it took Jacob less than an hour to claim his horse from the livery, stock up on his water and supplies, and hit the road, south and west into the desert.

CHAPTER THREE

Now, three days on the trail, Jacob was mad as a hornet and even more determined to get his man. He had followed the bank robber through flat terrain, around low hills, and between two small silver mines. Jacob all but lost the trail a couple times where miners' carts and mules' hoofprints obscured the track. Corker must have known he was being tailed; he'd tried to lose Jacob near the abandoned Espejo mine, covering his tracks and attempting misdirection. Once, Jacob had got close enough that the man had left his campfire burning in his haste to escape, but Jacob had just missed him.

Only once before had a wanted man eluded him so long, but Jacob didn't think this Corker fella was anything special.

Once he and Paint had climbed out of the riverbed up the opposite bank, Jacob mounted again. He nudged the horse forward, but it stepped sideways around the mouth of a burrow that the bounty hunter hadn't noticed, half hidden by the brittlebush overgrowth.

"Good job, boy," Jacob murmured to his mount. "You're smarter than me sometimes."

From his vantage atop the pinto, Jacob could see that the river curved around to the north of him. There was a small concentration of agave plants along the riverbed, extending about fifty feet to his left and curving back toward the hills where Jacob was heading. That was a good sign. Chances he'd find water in that canyon were much stronger if a river sometimes ran from it.

Jacob's mouth felt dry, and he was having trouble swallowing. He pulled out his canteen again and allowed himself a more full drink, coming closer to quenching his thirst yet still missing the mark. He drank again. He sensed he was close to the final confrontation with Corker and wanted to be ready. Full strength. Leave nothing to chance.

Jacob sat high above the flat terrain, in full view of anyone who might be watching. He held no hope of ambushing or surprising the outlaw. The man would be watching for him, no doubt, readying his gun or knife. Jacob's only course would be to overpower the man. He would like to be able to take him alive, but he knew that it might not be possible to walk away with both his own life and Corker's still intact.

He unhooked his hammer loop and pulled his revolver free, resting it carefully in one hand while he held the horse's reins with the other. Another quick nudge and Paint began walking forward, around the brittlebush and to the shady canyon up ahead. Jacob kept it slow; he needed to keep all his focus on the mouth of the canyon, eyes peeled for movement or activity, and let the horse take watch for animals and danger below.

Ten, twenty, forty feet through the brush, Paint brought Jacob closer to his target. He felt a rivulet of sweat running down the back of his head to his collar. At about twenty yards from the canyon, Jacob pulled back, pausing Paint's advance. He took a deep breath, breathing in through his nose and filling his lungs. The bounty hunter had always had a keen sense of smell, and he found that paying attention to slight variations in the air helped him more oft than not. There was a heavy, smoky touch woven into the dirt and light floral ahead.

A campfire, Jacob thought. Maybe he's cooking, or maybe he just put it out from this morning, but I smell wood burning.

He bent forward, close to the horse's mane, and looked again. No sign of movement up ahead, but that smell was an unmistakable sign.

"Once we get to the cool of that canyon, we'll rest, pal," Jacob promised, again nudging the horse forward. "We've got him cornered."

Jacob stopped again just five yards from the mouth of the canyon. The smell of burnt wood was even stronger here, and it didn't take him long to spot the source. Just to the right of the path was a small, still smoldering campfire.

Jacob eyed it with suspicion.

Why would anyone be burning a fire this late in the day, especially if that person was trying to stay hid? And why would someone on the run build a fire in such plain sight in the first place? The outlaw had already demonstrated he knew Jacob was following him; this campfire could be a trap, an ambush, or a distraction.

And Jacob wasn't aiming to get caught unawares.

Jacob pulled his eyes from the embers and scanned the interior of the canyon. About fifteen yards from the mouth, the walls began to get steep and almost vertical, and between here and there were taller bushes and even a couple trees. Harsh shadows stretched across the ground, and Jacob looked hard for evidence of another human being.

A tiny flash of light caught Jacob's eye. He turned Paint back around toward the mouth of the canyon and realized it was the glint of sun on steel.

"That you, Corker? You wanna make this easy or hard?"

Paint turned in a full circle, stepping around a barrel cactus, and Jacob lost sight of the steel barrel of the gun as he turned. If the outlaw was hiding out in this canyon, they both knew it was only a matter of time before Jacob would catch up with him.

"Corker!" he called again as he nudged Paint forward.

"Don't come any closer," a deep, gravely voice warned.

With the echo within the canyon walls, Jacob couldn't quite place where that voice was coming from. No further wink of gun showed in the sun.

"Give up, Corker," Jacob called. "I don't want to have to kill you."

A loud, hearty laugh answered him. "I warned you . . ." the stranger said, his voice trailing off. "You'll not be the one doing the killing."

Jacob leaned down to pet Paint's shoulder. "We got him, boy. Let's go."

The horse had only taken two more steps toward the canyon when Jacob heard the crack of gunfire, followed closely by the whinny of the pinto in pain. Before he could take another breath, he felt the animal collapse underneath him, falling, crumbling to the ground.

"Corker!" Jacob yelled into the canyon. His voice echoed and bounced off the rock, but he could still hear the rustle and crash of a man running through the wilderness. "You devil!"

His right leg was pinned under Paint, who lay on his side whimpering. Jacob didn't think his leg was any worse hurt than bruised, but the horse wouldn't be able to recover from that fatal blast.

The outlaw had shot the horse in his right shoulder, dropping the poor animal to the ground with Jacob still on top. Now footsteps raced away, echoing around the canyon. Jacob cursed under his breath—his mark was escaping . . . but he had to deal with the situation at hand first.

Jacob slowly, carefully, maneuvered his foot out from under the injured horse. The width of his boot was still wrapped in his stirrup. He had to twist his ankle to disentangle himself, driving the toe of his boot into the horse's ribs. Jacob cursed under his breath again, going slowly and trying not to hurt Paint any further.

He squatted before the horse, examining the wound where the bullet had embedded in the heavy muscle. Blood rivulets were already trailing down to the dust underneath the creature.

"Shhh . . ." Jacob whispered as he held his revolver to the horse's head. "I'm sorry, boy."

The horse whinnied again and Jacob's heart sank. Paint had been his companion ever since he left Texas and crossed over to the Arizona Territory, and he had hoped they'd still have years left together. The animal had helped him track and catch up with at least half of the outlaws Jacob had put in shackles. The poor beast deserved better than this death, alone in the dust and blood at the mouth of a nameless canyon.

Jacob closed his eyes as he squeezed the trigger. The crack of gunshot echoed through the canyon, and the horse's whinnies abruptly ceased.

After letting out a long, deep sigh, Jacob set to work rescuing his saddle, bags, canteen, and bedroll from Paint's corpse. He was three days' ride out from the closest town—how long would that be on foot? He shook the canteen. The contents sloshed around in the bottom of the leather container. Jacob estimated less than a quarter full. Enough for the rest of the day, but no longer.

Well, he thought with a sigh. At least he wouldn't need to share the water with Paint anymore.

When he was done, a pile of his necessities sat to the side of the path. What would he need to take with him as he proceeded on foot, and what could he leave behind? Jacob looked up and judged the position of the sun in the sky. With Corker so close, he waged he could capture that man and make it back here by nightfall. He would only carry what he needed to subdue the outlaw: rope, coiled tightly and slung over his shoulder; two revolvers, each with a bullet ready in the chamber; canteen of water, for when he found the spring he prayed would be back there; and a Bowie knife, tucked in his boot just in case.

As Jacob stood, still some yards from the mouth of the canyon, he felt exposed on the flat horizon. His gaze raked the shaded space between the hills, looking for any further sign of Corker, but found nothing. The man had already run deeper into the canyon.

Jacob began his cautious advance.

He walked past the smoldering campfire at the mouth of the canyon without giving it a second glance. There were no other signs or indications that a camp of any kind had been made here. Instead, Corker had apparently set up this small burning wood as a trap—a trap Jacob and Paint had walked right into. It was easy bait to lure in any lawman who might be following him and looking for signs of him. He'd then waited for his chance to incapacitate his pursuer.

Wherever Corker had gone, Jacob no longer heard him. No echo of footsteps or rumble of laughter reached his ears. He paused in the shade of a mesquite tree and readjusted his rope over his shoulder, then hiked up into the depths of the canyon.

It was another thirty feet into the canyon before Jacob noticed any other signs of the outlaw. It was easy to miss, but he spotted a set of footprints and the butt of a barely smoked cigarette down behind the large rocks jutting out of the side of the canyon wall. Jacob squatted down to take a closer look; judging from the print, it looked like Corker had also been squatting there on the balls of his feet, probably just waiting and watching for whatever lawman was on his trail.

Jacob smiled grimly to himself, pleased that he had so disturbed the other man's escape plans. The more Corker worried about what the bounty hunter was doing, the more chance there would be that he would slip up and make a mistake. Just judging from the man's errors so far, Jacob knew it was only a matter of time before he could push his clear-headed, even-keeled, patient advantage.

The cigarette still smoldered, so Jacob ground it into the dirt under his heel. There were many reasons Jacob didn't smoke; the fact that the dregs could give away his location was just one of them.

Corker's bootprints sprinted deeper into the canyon. Jacob sped up his tracking, following the clear path of Corker's down the middle of the ravine to where it turned around a bend on the right.

The canyon walls towered high above Jacob's head, forty feet above him and blocking out the sun. Ahead of him, the ravine curved to the right, parallel to Corker's footprints.

Jacob hurried his steps. Walking through the shade between the two hills immediately gave Jacob more energy, as short a respite it may be. He hadn't minded being in the direct sun for so long, but now that he was out of it, he could move faster and work harder without as much of a danger of losing all his water. Here, where the ground was still mostly even, where the dry riverbed transitioned into the level ground of the canyon, Jacob could almost set off at a run.

He turned the corner. The prints disappeared and the canyon broke into three separate paths.

Jacob paused, unsure of how to proceed.

CHAPTER FIVE

———

Three branches. Three choices. Three chances to be wrong in his guess where Jed Corker had got to.

Jacob took only a quick glance before choosing the middle path. The path on the left was dappled in cool shade from the trees; the path on the right was wide and bright, almost welcoming in its stillness. But the path in the middle was the darkest, the shadiest, and the narrowest. It was the most likely to dead-end, but also possibly the most likely to have more caves and corners to hide in and ambush someone from.

That's where Jacob would go if he were the man on the run.

He didn't slow his pace. Gripping the rope over his left shoulder and his revolver in his right hand, he took long, almost bouncing strides up the path. This narrow canyon had some corners and rocks that jutted out, and it seemed to get more confined the

farther he went. At times Jacob even had to turn sideways to fit his broad shoulders through the ravine. He
kept his eyes open for more clues to Corker's trail, but
kept moving forward.

His hurried steps and long legs helped him cover a
lot of ground quickly, so it was only about ten minutes
before he realized he was on the wrong path.

Jacob turned left around another bend in the
canyon, only to have to stop abruptly. He had found
himself at a dead end. The rock wall soared above his
head, smooth and unmarked by footholds—no indication that the other man had ever been here. The
bounty hunter pursed his lips, exhaling roughly in
frustration. He had guessed incorrectly.

"Dammit," he cursed to himself.

Corker kept slipping out of his grasp. The outlaw
had managed to increase his advantage simply
through Jacob's wrong assumption.

He backtracked to where the three branches of
the canyon began. Hands on hips, eyes scanning the
terrain, Jacob paused, unsure of how to proceed. He
was sure the outlaw's path had turned the corner into
this branch of the canyon, but *then* where had he
gone?

Jacob backed up a few steps to look again at the
footprints. Corker's boots plainly ran up the dirt path,
then stopped at the branch. He examined both walls
of the ravine, looking for signs the man had climbed
rather than run farther.

Not only was there no indication of anyone scaling
up the rock face, but Jacob didn't even see any indication that there were foot- or handholds that would aid

him in a climb up. The stone seemed moderately smoothed, worn down by centuries of water and wind coursing through this canyon. Experimentally, he tugged on the scraggly weed growing out of a crack. It easily came free of the dirt and into his hand. There were no good anchors to aid in a climb up the rock face.

Corker must have traveled deeper into the canyon on foot, but had hidden his footprints somehow.

Jacob was frustrated, flexing his hand into a fist. He took a deep breath and willed himself to think through this slowly, logically. He could sense he was close, and he just wanted to go tearing down one of the branches of the canyon to find his target, but if he chose wrong again he would have to backtrack and waste untold amounts of time.

He closed his eyes, imagining what he would do if he were Corker, how he would escape a tracker or erase the clues that pointed to his whereabouts.

Erase. That was it.

Jacob opened his eyes again and looked more carefully at the dust under his feet where the outlaw's footprints ended. There was a different quality to the ground here in the canyon than had been out in the desert or the riverbed. In fact—he looked again—there was a different quality here than was even in the first part of the canyon. It almost seemed to have brushstrokes in the dirt.

He stepped to the edge of the path, careful not to disturb the pattern on the ground, and stalked ahead, totally focused on the dirt beneath him. There was a very clear pattern of sweeping back and forth. Jacob suspected that Corker had used a branch of shrub or tree to wipe out evidence of his footprints behind him as he progressed. But here the joke fell on Corker: the sweeping marks themselves were enough of a track for Jacob.

Once he knew what to look for, the outlaw's path was obvious. Jacob traced the erasing pattern from where the ravine turned, down toward the branch of canyon on the right, and another twenty yards, until the tree branch he had used was discarded on the side of the canyon and the bootprints resumed.

Jacob snorted, holding in his laughter. Corker was lazy. He may have learned some tricks from Elliott "Slippery" Stone on how to escape, but he wasn't as thorough or committed as he should be. That would be his downfall.

Now that he was positive he was on the correct trail, Jacob hurried his tracking again. He shook his head in wonder at Corker's choice. There was nowhere in this fork of the canyon to hide, not even any plants or boulders in this stretch. His bootprints were plain as day in the dirt floor, as though calling for Jacob to follow him.

The canyon curved slowly around to the left, where small boulders lay strewn across the path.

Jacob stepped up into the narrow path between the boulders.

A rattle arrested his next movement.

The rattle soon became two, three, and innumerable rattles echoing all about him. He looked around. His heart began pounding as he realized he had stepped directly into a nest of rattlesnakes.

CHAPTER SIX

The rattling noise grew louder, more insistent, and the first of the diamondbacks showed itself to Jacob. Slithering forward from the shadow of the nearby boulder, the three-foot-long reptile reared back, baring its venomous fangs.

He'd heard tell that these snakes were the few that would stand their ground, instead of slither away and hide. Jacob's palms began to sweat, his body on high alert against the death threat.

A second rattlesnake caught his eye, hissing at him from the path straight ahead.

He had only been in the Arizona Territory for a year, not quite long enough that rattlesnake encounters were common for him. Back in Virginia, where he grew up, he knew how to handle the dangerous copperhead or water moccasin, but rattlesnakes were a new threat.

A third and fourth rattlesnake slithered into his view, from underneath the dry shrub in this corner of the canyon. He froze, hand on his revolver, unsure how to proceed.

He knew—he *thought*—the snakes would only come at him if they felt threatened. They probably wouldn't chase him. He froze where he stood, weighing his options. Each second he stayed unmoving was another second Jed Corker could take to get farther away.

More and more of the deadly snakes made themselves heard. The echoing of the rattles became a crescendo, surrounding Jacob. He spun slowly, finding reptiles in all directions alert and warning him of their menace.

Jacob thought back to what he had been taught about rattlesnakes from the locals since arriving in Arizona: that he likely wouldn't be bothered much by them. He hadn't thought to ask what to do in the unlikely event he *was* bothered by them. He hadn't thought it would be so easy to surprise an entire nest of the things. He assumed that he'd been making enough noise to warn them of his approach to let them get away. The animals shouldn't be seeking him out like this.

Something wasn't right here.

Jacob slowly wrapped his fingers around the coil of rope slung over his left shoulder. Grasping it in one hand, he lowered the cord so it was hanging from his fist, nearer to the ground. As one of the snakes made to attack, Jacob used the rope to block the lunge. The rattlesnake's fangs sunk into the rope instead of Jacob's calf.

As the snake shook itself loose, he noticed a

disturbance in the dirt around it. Behind the crowd of snakes, there was a trail in the dirt where stones had rolled or slid. They were out of place. The ground here was almost totally flat—why would a stone have moved on its own?

As another snake reared up to hiss at him, Jacob seethed.

This was another trap that Corker had set up for him. Somehow the outlaw had riled up the snakes, putting them on guard—likely after he had already passed the nest and just before Jacob would walk into it. Maybe he tossed a rock or otherwise harassed them out of their burrow, just in time for them to be on the defensive when Jacob made his way through.

He knew he couldn't do anything but wait. There was no going around them, and he couldn't go back. Jacob could only stand still and hope that the mess of rattlers would give up shortly and that Corker wouldn't get too far ahead in the meantime.

Jacob holstered his revolver. Shooting a snake seemed impractical, but his Bowie knife would be a more likely defense in case they did come after him.

As he reached down to his boot, Jacob noticed a stirring out of the corner of his eye. His movement had startled one of the largest rattlesnakes. It lunged forward. Jacob grasped for the hilt of the Bowie knife, but the snake was faster. Before he knew it, the venomous fangs had sunk deep into his right forearm.

Jacob grunted in pain, but managed to wrap his fingers around the knife's handle. In one swift move-ment, he shook the snake loose and swiped his knife straight across, severing the snake's head from its body before it reached the ground.

He moved the knife to his left hand. He could feel the venom already sinking into his bloodstream. He used the blade to cut back the fabric of his shirt, revealing two small puncture wounds where the fangs had pierced his skin, releasing their deadly defense.

Jacob knew what he had to do—though he had never attempted such a thing.

To his left was a small boulder, about knee-high. With the small bit of strength he still had, Jacob stepped up to the top of it. He would wait out the snakes' fury from here—provided he didn't collapse under the effects of the venom.

He kept his injured arm steady and tried to breathe calm into his thumping heart. Any movement or panic would encourage the blood to pump and send the venom deeper into his bloodstream. With his free hand he patted down his pockets, finally finding what he was looking for in the pocket on his backside: a narrow strip of leather, the strap he had been using to keep his bedroll tied to the saddle. Awkwardly, quickly as he could with one hand, he wrapped the strip around his bicep, tying a clumsy knot and pulling the leather tight with his teeth.

He gasped inadvertently at the pain. The leather cuff cut off his blood circulation even further, but Jacob could feel the effects of the venom already building. He blinked several times in rapid succession, trying to see past the encroaching double vision.

His hand shook as he brought the sharp point of his Bowie knife to his arm. A small *X* incision at the point of the bite gave him a target, but the pain of it almost made his knees buckle.

With the sleeve clear of the wound, Jacob brought his arm to his mouth and swiftly sucked the venom out. He spat the bloody mouthful to the ground and brought his arm up again. It took four times total for Jacob to feel like he might have gotten as much of the venom out as he could. Losing blood at the same time he was low on water made him lightheaded, but he managed to stay on his feet.

Though the rattling had abated somewhat, Jacob was still surrounded by at least a dozen rattlesnakes, still angry and defending their territory. He moved the knife back to his weakened right hand and pulled his canteen from the strap over his shoulder. After fumbling with the cap, Jacob carefully poured a small bit of water onto his wound.

He hissed at the pain; the water almost burned as it cleaned out the punctures. He didn't have anything to bandage his arm other than the already ripped sleeve, but he couldn't take time to do that as long as he was still surrounded by rattlesnakes.

He felt lightheaded. He must not have gotten all the venom, but he didn't trust himself to try again. Jacob spread his feet apart, trying to balance more evenly on top of the boulder. A wave of nausea crept over him. He fought it as long as he could, then vomited onto the ground before him. The little water he had let himself drink that day now lay in a puddle in the dirt.

The reptiles were beginning to lose interest, and the closer ones recoiled from the liquid splashing in the dirt. Jacob took a deep breath and steeled himself. He couldn't wait all day for the snakes to scatter, but he also couldn't trust himself to get past them in this state.

He stood up straight again, watching the remaining rattlers warily. His knees began to shake a bit, and Jacob knew he couldn't last as he was much longer. Not if his body was going to be able to fight off the infection and trace amounts of venom. He reluctantly opened his canteen and downed most of the remaining water.

If he didn't find more water in the canyon, he didn't know how he would get himself back to Tucson —with or without the outlaw.

As the last diamondback slithered into its den, Jacob stepped carefully down off the boulder. He looked ahead to the path and for more clues of Corker. The outlaw had succeeded in derailing Jacob's hunt more than once—even injuring him in the process—but he must be running out of tricks.

Just like Jacob was running out of water.

Jacob pulled his canteen off the strap on his shoulder and treated himself to just a single mouthful, nearly emptying the container. His body cried out for water after losing so much sweat in the previous days, and he knew he could only go so much farther without severe repercussions.

He opened and closed his right fist experimentally. Would that small movement send the rattlesnake's venom deeper into his bloodstream? Jacob still felt nauseated and lightheaded. The muscles of his forearm burned around the bite mark, but at this point he didn't seem to be getting any worse. What he mostly needed was a hot meal and rest. Unfortunately, those were the last things he could have right now. If he took one more break, Jed Corker could get away, likely to continue his attacks on innocent people throughout the region.

The path ahead of Jacob was straight and clear—for this section of canyon, at least. He hadn't actually seen another human in days. He usually enjoyed his time in the desert, but this time he was ready to get back. As he continued his pursuit, the bounty hunter remembered the last time he had been so many days into the wilderness.

Back before he left Virginia, he would deliberately take several days away from his land to be alone in the Blue Ridge Mountains. The first couple times, his wife hadn't understood why he wanted to leave her; but as time wore on she began to see how much those days by himself in the wild restored him.

He missed her. And if she had lived through the war and had come west with him, she'd be scolding him something fierce for his negligence on this trail. The difference, of course, was that Jacob could always find water in the Blue Ridge Mountains. Water was everywhere in Virginia. He hadn't thought he would miss it as much as he did at this moment.

Jacob was startled out of his reminiscing by a heavy thudding sound high above him. He looked up swiftly, trying to identify the sound, just in time to see a piece of the canyon wall crumble. A cloud of dirt puffed out where something—a bird? a stone?—hit the jutting-out corner of canyon wall and broke it off. Jacob watched, fascinated, before he grasped what was happening.

As high above him as it was, Jacob hadn't realized just how large the rocky slice of canyon wall was until it was plummeting toward him. Jacob dove to the ground, but it was too little too late. The huge stone crashed into him, jutting hard into his shoulder and ripping his pack from his back, before rolling farther down the canyon.

He groaned into the dirt. That would be another bruise, maybe worse. This hunt was proving to be more physically demanding than he had expected. It would be worth it when he brought in Jed Corker, though.

Jacob rolled onto his back, preparing to get to his feet again, when a panicked thought flashed through his head.

He had rolled onto his back.

He shouldn't be able to roll onto his back.

He should have a canteen strapped there.

He sat up, fully panicked, looking around, and saw his canteen six feet away, where the stone had ripped it from his back, the cap fallen off and the last drops of his water supply dripping into the dirt.

"No!" he exclaimed, scrambling on his knees to the canteen. He caught up the leather bag and was immediately dismayed. There was no weight, no telltale sloshing.

The last of his water was gone.

He punched his fist into the dirt in frustration; the pain shot through his already injured arm.

No more water.

He was completely out of water, with who knew how many days of travel in the sun ahead of him, if he couldn't catch Corker soon. This canyon showed signs of foliage, so maybe there was a chance he'd find water. But only a chance. This was the desert, after all.

Now Jacob's best hope was to find Corker and

pray the other man still had a supply of water to maintain the both of them.

He pulled himself to his feet and took a deep breath.

If anyone could do this, it was Jacob Payne, bounty hunter.

He began his hike again, deeper into the canyon. The path narrowed ahead, turning slightly to the right. Jacob closed the final steps to meet the unknown around the corner.

CHAPTER EIGHT

Just before he rounded the corner, another familiar scent arrested Jacob's progress. He paused and sniffed again.

For a bounty hunter on the trail in the west, the stench was as common as coffee, and in this case just as welcome. He breathed it in: manure. There was a horse nearby. A horse that would carry him outta here once he'd completed his mission. Like as not, it was Corker's horse, which meant the outlaw himself would also be close.

Jacob crept up around the bend, his back to the wall of the canyon, his hand ready on his revolver to draw if need be. As he peeked around the rock, he spotted the source of the stench.

A dapple gray horse stood near the right wall of the canyon, its reins tied off on the overhanging branch of a mesquite tree. Jacob waited and watched for at least a minute, to be sure, but the horse seemed more or less content. And alone. Its owner was nowhere in sight.

Jacob crept up to the horse, slowly, in case Corker was watching from some unseen location.

"Whoa there, buddy," Jacob said under his breath, one hand outstretched to touch the horse. "You all alone? You okay?" The palm of his hand flat against the horse's neck, Jacob soothed the animal, which had been spooked by his approach.

He looked around, certain he'd find another clue as to the outlaw's whereabouts.

Just a few yards past where the horse stood, the ravine narrowed farther, and huge boulders filled the width of the canyon. The first stood as high as Jacob's chest, and offered no clear path over or around. Jacob could barely picture a man climbing up through the canyon over those rocks, let alone a horse.

When he turned back to Corker's ride, he noticed another reason that the animal had been abandoned here. The tiniest trickle of water dripped down from the crack in the wall of the canyon. There was enough output from this spring to puddle down near Jacob's feet, and he recognized the heel of a boot in the mud leading away, farther up the canyon toward the boulders.

Another clue that Corker had been here.

Jacob grinned to himself. He was closing in. He made a quick plan: He would add some water to his canteen and then continue his hunt. He could leave the horse waiting for when he brought Corker back through the canyon. It wouldn't be long before he found the outlaw's camp. He couldn't go far without his horse, nor could he go away from the only source of water for miles.

After visually searching the canyon again, Jacob reluctantly returned his Bowie knife to the sheathe in his boot and used both hands to maneuver the canteen into place. His left hand was needed to support his weakened right arm.

Once he helped himself to the first few gulps of water, Jacob settled in to fill the canteen for the rest of his hunt. In only a few short minutes, though, he realized he had to change his plan. With such a small output, it would take far too long for Jacob to fill his gallon leather canteen. He elected to fill it halfway now, then again on his way out of the canyon once he had captured Corker. He'd be stopping to claim the horse, and could spend the night in this spot.

He paused for a moment, letting the fresh water course through his system. Even just this small amount was helping. His lightheadedness was clearing and he was feeling more stable on his feet. He could keep moving toward the outlaw.

Once his new water supply was stored away and again strapped over his shoulder, Jacob took a deep breath and assessed the rocks in front of him. This must be where Corker continued up into the canyon, scrambling over boulders, or maybe even squeezing into hiding places between them like the snake he was.

With as much gear as he could carry strapped to his back, Jacob had a slight struggle to climb on top of the first boulder. He almost lost his hat when he had to bend so far forward to get a solid grip on the rock.

His right arm around the snakebite twinged, but he didn't let that stop him.

The sole of his boot skidded only once on the smooth surface of stone. When Jacob reached the top of the first boulder, he stood upright and surveyed the path before him. Ahead were more boulders to climb over, but there seemed to be another stretch of clear ground in about ten yards. If he could keep his feet under him, he'd be up the canyon in just a couple minutes.

He felt something cool fall on his hand and immediately looked up for a bird or plant on the cliff above. No movement caught his eye. There was no signal as to what had dropped on him, until Jacob noticed the blue sky above was gone. He had gotten used to the lack of sun, being deep in the canyon for so long, but when he looked up he realized that a thick gray cloud covered the sky at the top of the ravine.

The storm he had been warned about had arrived. Raindrops fell slowly at first, peppering his sleeves with wet spots here and there.

Jacob laughed out loud, his chuckle echoing against the walls.

Water. It was water. For as many days as he had been looking for water, for as careful as he had been to not run out of it early and not put himself in danger, now it was raining.

And right after he had found a spring.

Rain in the desert.

Jacob lifted his face to the sky. Cool drops of water the size of silver dollars dropped gently on his face. He closed his eyes and opened his mouth, letting the water fall over him. He leaned so far back, his hat fell completely off this time. He caught it but let the cool rain stream down over his head and his hair and down to his collar.

The rain started to fall heavily.

Then, Jacob heard the bone-shaking crack of thunder.

CHAPTER NINE

Thunder rolled through the canyon. Jacob felt it in his bones. Lightning flashed, another crack of thunder following only two seconds later. The storm had closed in on him before he'd realized it was coming. How had he missed it? Wind whipped around him, racing though the canyon. He slammed his hand to his head, holding his hat in place. Being this deep in the canyon, surrounded by stone walls on all sides, Jacob hadn't even noticed the drop in temperature or the increased humidity.

All thought of capturing Corker was forgotten while Jacob prioritized what he needed to do to prepare for the coming downpour. He holstered his revolver, protecting it from the wet as much as he could.

Lightning flashed again, the thunder rumble immediately following. This storm—monsoon, they called it here—was right on top of him. He had no chance to find shelter and would have to ride out the rain as best he could.

The boulder under his feet was beginning to get slick with water. The sole of his boot slipped again and Jacob stumbled a little to keep his balance. Where could he move? If he climbed down again, he'd be stuck in the mud as more rain fell. But could he climb up to the next higher boulder with all the slickness? Should he even attempt it?

The rain came faster now, thicker, obscuring his sight. Jacob used the back of his hand to wipe the water from his eyes, blinking rapidly. The brim of his hat couldn't stop the sheet of water falling from the sky. The rope coiled around his shoulder began to feel heavier as it soaked through.

His foot glided over the surface of the boulder, and this time he wasn't able to regain his balance under the weight and strength of the relentless rain. The boot slid forward and out from under him, and as Jacob fell his lower back smashed against the boulder he had just been standing on.

"Argh!" he cried, the pain surprising him. Jacob arched his back, landing hard on the pack of supplies and just keeping his head from also cracking on the rock. As he tumbled, he felt the muscle on his back bruise almost immediately. He crumpled to the now-muddy ground at the foot of the boulder, water rising around him.

In what had been the simple pursuit of an outlaw, Jacob had been battered from all sides and now ached all over. The water rushed down over the boulders, pouring over him where he lay on the ground. While his hat kept the water off his face for the moment, every other inch of Jacob was soaked. The ground beneath him softened into mud quickly, his weight sinking deeper every second. He braced himself against the side of the boulder, struggling to pull himself to standing under the sheer strength of the water now pouring onto him from the flow over the rocks.

He had never seen a flash flood. The mellow hills of Virginia spread out any influx of rain, the many rivers and creeks quickly draining into the Atlantic Ocean. Even the strongest storms weren't enough to fill a Virginian valley this quickly. But the focused narrowness of this canyon, the hard rock that denied any absorption, directed the full downpour straight toward Jacob.

Somewhere farther upstream, Jed Corker must have been barely hanging on himself.

Jacob couldn't keep his feet under him in this current. He couldn't afford to lose any ground or time. He needed to anchor himself and find a way to hold his own so he could cross this flood and get farther up the canyon to nab his target.

He looked up the canyon, blinking into the sheet of water, past the boulder he had just fallen from, and spied the nearly petrified stump of a tree. It was at least twenty feet up the canyon, across the quickly forming river rushing down toward him. That was it. His anchor. A tree that size should have deep, strong roots, and if Jacob could get a solid grip, he could wait out the storm holding tight to that.

He pulled his hat down farther on his head, tight,

praying it wouldn't blow off while his hands were otherwise busy. The rope was soaked through, its weight digging into his shoulder. He hadn't yet had much practice tying slip knots and lassoing, but he would have to make it work.

The first knot fell apart completely. Jacob's fingers must have slipped in the rain; he hadn't made the loops correctly, or he didn't pull the rope tight enough. He wasn't sure where he went wrong, so he shook it apart and started over. He bent forward a little more to keep the rain out of his face, but the water pouring off the brim of his hat formed a veritable curtain around him.

"Drat," he muttered under his breath, and started again.

He tied the loose knot, pulled the end through, paused to shake more rain out of his face, tightened it, and finished up his lasso.

He took a deep breath and looked for the tree again, almost falling under the pour of rain. The thick clouds rolling in had completely obscured the sun, and the heavy shadows made it difficult to see too far in front of him.

Jacob could almost laugh. All them Tucson locals had been right to warn him.

A flash of lightning brightened the ravine for a split second and Jacob spied his target. Swinging the rope above his head, Jacob winced at the pain in his arm. He needed to put more effort and power behind it to counter the downpour.

His first throw was short, so he hurried to pull the rope back toward him.

He tried again, fighting through the pain and the rain to swing the rope above his head and propel it toward the tree. He held his breath for the two seconds before the loop landed over the top of the stump.

Jacob grasped the rope with both hands and pulled hard. The rope tightened around the stump.

He had his anchor. Now he just had to pull himself to it.

Jacob could barely hang on to the rope in this torrent. The coarse, wet fiber cut into his hands. How would he keep moving up the canyon? The longer he struggled, the longer Corker had to get away.

No sooner had Jacob secured his rope around the tree stump than lightning flashed, thunder rolled, and the storm intensified yet again. The current of water filling the canyon continued to rise at an alarming rate.

This was the flash flood he had been warned about.

Just as he took his first step back up onto the wet boulder, he lost his footing. Holding on to the rope, he found himself being swung this way and that in the flow, his body slamming into the boulder. After a few hard crashes against the rock, Jacob got his body pointing the right direction and, both hands on the rope, planted the soles of his boots against the side of the boulder.

Hand over hand, Jacob clung tightly to his rope, step by step up the side of the boulder. The water, combined with the thread of the rope, began wearing down the skin of his hands. His palms burned, and as the water below him pulled his body in every direction, the tugging and rubbing on his hands wore through. He couldn't tell if water or blood was dripping down his wrist, or both. But still he held on.

With the help of the rope, Jacob climbed back up the boulder. His boots slipped over and over again, unable to get purchase under the rushing water, but he managed to pull himself up.

Strength. Willpower. Adrenaline.

He needed to keep moving, to keep pursuing his target. His right forearm still ached, but still he held on.

Once he reached the top of the boulder again, he didn't linger. Jacob wrapped the rope more securely around his wrist and stepped off the high point and into the water on the other side.

The current crushed his body against the rock, but he was determined. He couldn't even feel the ground under his feet, but he used his arms to pull himself forward, farther up the rope, closer to the tree stump that would be his safe haven.

Jacob risked a look up the canyon to see how far he still had to go, but almost immediately he had to lower his head again. He let go of the rope with one hand to clamp his hat to his head. If he lost that, he'd have a long, hot travel back to Tucson with no shade from the sun.

There were three more sizable boulders between Jacob and his end goal. Three more places he could be smashed and bounced around in the current. He kept moving. Hand over hand, palm slick with water and blood, his fingers cramping in their death grip.

Another man might have given up long ago, but not Jacob Payne. Every foot closer to the outlaw was progress, and he would not let himself rest. Forward along his drenched rope he went, until he finally climbed up to the petrified tree stump sitting above the waterline on the side of the canyon.

Jacob closed his eyes and wrapped the rope around his arm, and his arm around the tree, to secure himself. Water gushed toward him from all directions. Rain still burst from the sky, while more streams spilled off the canyon wall next to him, splashing onto his hat brim and shoulders. The floodwaters rushing over the boulders were as high as his knees now.

Under the roar of the storm, Jacob started laughing. He couldn't even hear himself, but he couldn't help but laugh, a full-throated laugh up into the storm-drenched sky. After three days of struggling and rationing, when every thought was of making his water supply last as long as possible, now the water was his biggest threat. Now all he wanted was for the water to stop.

As he laughed, Jacob thought he heard another laugh from elsewhere in the canyon, before he realized it was his own laughter's echo.

He could hear it. He could hear himself again.

He looked up to the sky, blinking against the falling rain, and realized the clouds were moving on. The storm was abating. There was no telling when the floodwaters would fully subside, but at least Jacob knew there wouldn't be more water.

Jacob fished his nearly empty canteen from the strap on his back and bent to refill it from the flash flood still rushing over his ankles. The added weight on his own back instead of a horse's might slow him down, but having enough water for his journey back was worth it.

Jacob took one last drink of water before he went on. He pulled his rope from the tree stump, still knotted, and coiled it in a loop to drape over his shoulder.

His gaze scanned the surface of the water as the flood receded. The storm had likely washed away all of Corker's trail, so he would have to start all over again. But that wouldn't be any trouble. If Corker moved, if Corker even breathed, Jacob would know it, and he would find him. There was only one direction he could be.

Jacob secured his canteen over his shoulder again and jumped down from his ledge into the ankle-deep water. It splashed around his boots as he took the first few tentative steps in the muddy path.

Jacob began running up the canyon. Now that he was past the boulders the ground had only a slight incline, and he made quick progress. He would catch up with Corker and surprise the man before he had even realized the storm had passed.

The ravine curved again around to the left a few yards ahead. As he ran around the bend, Jacob spotted movement—something dark gray and out of place—to the far right up ahead. He paused, hand reflexively on his gun. The thing was bobbing slightly, and as he crept closer Jacob realized what it was—a Stetson.

Corker had lost his hat, the idiot.

Jacob left it where it was; he might let the outlaw retrieve it once he'd been subdued, but for now it simply served as a confirmation that Jacob was close. He was on the murderer's trail and would soon bring this chase to a close.

He may have thrown all manner of obstacles at the bounty hunter, but like many outlaws, Corker had underestimated him to his downfall.

After he passed the outlaw's hat sinking in the mud, Jacob slowed his advance. Corker would be close, and he didn't want to come upon the murderer unawares. The man had already tried to shake his trail several times and had attempted to kill him several more. There was every reason to suspect he'd be waiting for the bounty hunter in ambush. He was dangerous and unstable, and Jacob would need every advantage to take him in to meet justice.

The canyon narrowed ahead of him and Jacob couldn't see beyond the tight passageway. He paused and took a deep breath, readying himself for battle. The floodwaters had completely abated, leaving just mud underfoot. He lowered his coil of rope and pack of supplies to the ground, lightening his load and making himself more limber for whatever Corker had waiting for him.

Jacob needed to know what waited for him beyond the bend. He doubled back to pick up Corker's hat and sidled flat along the side of the canyon. At the turn in the passageway, he decided on a quick experiment: he held out Corker's hat into view.

One revealing crack after another sounded, echoing around the stone, as three rapid gunshots pierced the brim of the dark gray Stetson. Jacob pulled the prop back before his hand got blown off.

It was an ambush, just as he suspected. Corker was just the sort of man who would get the jump on another, murdering innocent bank tellers and now shooting at what he thought was Jacob without warning.

Jacob always preferred to take in his targets alive, but if Corker wanted a fight, he would get one.

Jacob thought back, counting. That was three shots at the hat, and another at Paint at the start of the canyon. If he hadn't reloaded, Corker only had a couple shots left. Jacob would have to press his advantage quickly, before the other man rearmed himself. He stayed completely still, not making a sound to give away his presence. For all the outlaw knew, he had hit and killed the lawman trailing him.

Jacob listened as hard as he could around the turn in the canyon. The shuffle of footsteps told him Corker was only a few yards away. He reached down to arm himself with the Bowie knife from his boot. He was not a man to kill if he didn't have to. Whatever he found around the bend, Jacob wouldn't be shooting the other man in the back.

More sounds of feet moving back and forth, and Jacob thought Corker sounded anxious, unsteady. That meant he'd probably be on alert and waiting for

Jacob. He'd have to wait it out and give the outlaw time to let down his guard.

Jacob pressed his back to the stone wall and breathed as shallowly as he could. He'd wait forever if need be. He waited so long his pants had begun to dry from the flood. If there was one advantage Jacob had over most outlaws, it was patience. These wild men with their need for immediate gratification—robbing a bank instead of earning an honest living—could never out-wait the bounty hunter.

After an untold period of time, Corker had been quiet long enough that Jacob felt that the other man had the advantage. Whatever sounds Jacob's first movement made would give him away, so he'd have to take Corker in one swift movement.

In one long step, Jacob was around the bend in the canyon and facing Jed Corker. The outlaw, lanky with stringy blond hair hanging limply around his face, was leaning against the canyon wall, gun in hand, but stood up straight when he saw the bounty hunter.

"Hands up, Corker," Jacob cried.

The outlaw chuckled and shot. Jacob saw the movement and ducked back behind the cover of rock just in time. One more shot down. He was close to being able to overpower Corker.

"You don't have a chance, boy," he said, coming back around the rock. He stalked toward Corker, a weapon in each hand.

Corker aimed again, but Jacob didn't have time to take cover. The gun jammed and the outlaw cursed his luck while frantically trying shake something lose. Jacob grinned. He had seen it before. Men like this who thought they were invincible never took the time on basic things like gun cleaning.

He took several steps forward, aiming to take down Corker while he was distracted, but the other man looked up at the last second. He raised his revolver above his head, bringing it down toward Jacob's temple.

Bowie knife in his left hand, Jacob swiped at Corker, slicing the man across the wrist and deep into the meaty flesh of his thumb. The outlaw cried out in pain, dropping his gun in the process. Jacob wasted no time in kicking the weapon across the canyon floor and thrusting his own revolver at Corker.

"Hands in the air, you devil," Jacob said in a low, threatening tone.

The outlaw glowered at Jacob as he raised his hands in surrender, blood dripping down and staining his sleeve.

"That's right, Corker," Jacob said, pointing his revolver at the outlaw's chest. "Nice and slow, and maybe you'll live to see another day."

Once he was sure there would be no sudden moves, Jacob sheathed his Bowie knife and picked up Corker's pistol from the dirt at his feet. The knife went back in his boot and the gun went in his holster, while his own revolver stayed in his hand.

"Move. Now."

He gestured with the gun, and Corker shuffled forward a couple steps back up the ravine toward the narrow passageway. His hat lay in the mud where Jacob had left it.

"Pick it up," Jacob commanded.

He didn't take his eyes off the outlaw, tense and ready for any attempt at escape, while he bent down to retrieve his Stetson. Sitting just a few feet farther was the coil of rope and supplies Jacob had left behind. With the gun trained on the outlaw, Jacob used one foot, stuck it under the coil, and lifted his leg just high enough to be able to grab the rope without bending down and leaving himself vulnerable to the other man.

Corker glared at him.

"Hands in the air, I said."

Corker spat at Jacob; the glob of phlegm landed only inches from Jacob's feet, but he raised his hands again, high above his head.

"Now," Jacob said calmly. "Pick up this pack."

Corker glared but complied.

Jacob continued, "I'm gonna come over there and I'm gonna tie this rope around your wrists. You best not do anything stupid, now."

Corker didn't respond, but slowly lowered his hands. The two men eyed each other as the armed bounty hunter slowly, cautiously made his way across the several feet between them.

The look in the bank robber's eye made Jacob wary. He didn't trust this man as far as he could spit. Sure enough, as soon as Jacob got close enough, Corker kicked up his leg, aiming to disarm him. In a flash, Jacob fired the revolver. At this close range he hit exactly where he was aiming. Corker's left sleeve darkened in a bloom of blood where the bullet hit its mark.

"You—" Corker's litany of cursing was lost among his groans of pain.

"Can't say I didn't warn you."

With Corker so distracted, Jacob easily subdued him and bound his wrists together, further wrapping the rope tightly around the other man's arms. Corker yelped as Jacob pulled the knot tight.

"That'll have to do you for a bandage till we get somewhere," Jacob said. "I suggest you don't delay our travelin' any more than you have to."

With the tail end of the rope in one hand and his revolver in the other, Jacob had successfully protected the citizens of neighboring towns from this godless outlaw.

"Move," Jacob said, gesturing toward the mouth of the canyon with his gun.

Corker glared at him. For several breathless seconds, Jacob wasn't sure the captive would obey.

"I really prefer to take you alive," Jacob said casually. "But I don't particularly have to."

Corker heaved a giant sigh and turned to lead the way out of the canyon. He had a bit of trouble climbing over the high boulders with his wrists tied, but Jacob let him take as long as he needed.

When they reached the outlaw's horse, Corker sidled on up to the animal's side as if to make it known it was his property.

Jacob tied the end of the rope to the saddle, securing the knot and tugging experimentally.

"You ain't riding my horse," Corker griped.

"I sure as shootin' am," Jacob replied. "You shouldn'ta killt my horse if you didn't want me to take yours. Besides, the way I hear it, you stole this horse and it ain't yours anyway."

Using the barrel of his revolver, he gestured again at where he wanted Corker to go.

"You walk on ahead, now. I'll not be turning my

back to you or untying you at any point. I know your tricks now, Corker, and you'll not be slipping away from me this time."

Corker called him all manner of names under his breath as he shuffled on ahead.

Jacob watched him carefully as he mounted the dapple gray and began the walk back to the mouth of the canyon. Corker dragged his feet, but a periodic poke in the back with the toe of his boot and Jacob had him moving again.

Valleseco was closer than Tucson, only about a day's ride from where they were in the desert. He'd take Corker there and let the bank and the sheriff decide what to do with him. They had two full canteens of water and at least three hours of daylight left before they needed to make camp. Jacob ignored the outlaw's complaining and kept his eyes looking up —up toward the sun, and toward the lawmen they'd meet the next day.

JUSTICE FOR JASPER

CHAPTER ONE

Jacob Payne almost got himself bit.

"Whoa, there!" He pulled his fingers away just in time. The dapple gray mustang had seemed friendly enough, but as soon as Jacob's fingers brushed close to its mouth, it snapped at him. Jacob glared at the horse's current owner. "Thought you said this one was broken."

Caleb Shaw widened his eyes, wearing his most innocent expression. "He is. You musta riled him somehow."

"Uh huh," Jacob muttered.

He turned back to examine the horse, keeping out of reach of its strong jaw—which was no way to really learn anything, but he kept trying. Jacob needed to have something to ride out of there today.

The bounty hunter's previous horse, Paint, had been shot from under him while he was on the trail of a bank robber out in the desert. In the several days since he captured Jed Corker and turned him over to the lawful authorities, he had managed to do without a horse of his own, staying in town and going everywhere on foot.

But now, looking at Shaw's meager selection, Jacob wondered how much longer he could do without. It's not that he couldn't afford a fine horse, but more that there were none to be had. His current options were a mare that had given birth two days earlier, a Morgan that could not be younger than twenty years, or this one with the biting—Shaw called him Smoke. Jacob wondered how he'd manage to bridle the creature without losing his fingers.

"You sure you don't have any others for sale, Shaw?" Jacob asked, turning back to the the man.

"Payne, I swear—"

"Jacob Payne!" a big voice shouted from the doorway of the livery. "Anyone seen Payne?"

"Who's asking?" Jacob shouted back. Shielding his eyes against the sunny backdrop, Jacob made out the silhouette of a tall, thin man walking toward him. Out here in Arizona Territory, a stranger knowing his name could either be very good or very bad.

"U.S. Marshal Owen Santos," the man said as he approached.

As the stranger got closer, Jacob noticed he was holding up a badge. From this distance he couldn't make out what the badge said, but he'd heard of Santos all right.

"I'm Jacob Payne. What can I do for you, Marshal?"

Santos took off his hat and offered his hand to the bounty hunter. The Marshal stood taller than

Jacob by several inches, which was uncommon, but was leaner than a bean pole. Jacob's broad shoulders could probably hide the other man behind him twice over.

He shook the marshal's hand, then noticed Shaw awkwardly watching the interaction.

"Have you met Caleb Shaw, Marshal?" he asked, gesturing.

The lawman glanced at the livery owner, barely acknowledging him before turning his attention back to Jacob. "I'm gonna tell you this straight. I need your help. I can legally force you into helping, but I'd rather you come willingly."

Jacob was half defensive and half amused by this approach. Though he wasn't technically a man of the law, he still respected what men like Santos had to do. "What is it you need, sir?"

Santos let out a deep sigh and rolled his eyes. His annoyance rolled off of him in waves. "Well, seems the sheriff down in Jasper can't do the job he was elected to do. He's called on the marshal's office for assistance, and all my men are out in the field."

"Assistance with what?"

"Claims he's identified a wanted murderer, one Floyd Daly. But seeing as the man is currently in the employ of the Rockville Mining Company, he's having a devil of a time even getting close to him."

"You need me to go down and capture this Daly character?"

"Oh, I don't mind goin' down there to collect the man myself, but I don't dare trust the sheriff to back me up if I need it. I need a capable associate by my side if things go south. You're the first person I thought of."

"Why me?"

"All I been hearin' these last few months is 'Jacob Payne *this*' and 'Jacob Payne *that*.' You've made quite the impression since you arrived in Arizona. Bonnie, in particular, seems to like the taste of your name in her mouth."

Jacob smiled. Bonnie, his favorite waitress at the San Xavier Cafe just a few blocks away, sure did make his visits to Tucson pleasant. But she couldn't be the only one talking about him to the U.S. Marshal. Likely the sheriffs of Bennettsville or Valleseco—or maybe even San Adrian, if they had a new sheriff already—would be speaking well of him.

"I'm happy to help if I can, Marshal."

"Much obliged. I'll deputize you now and we'll be on our way tomorrow morning."

"One problem, sir. I still don't have a horse—"

"Since Jed Corker shot yours? Yeah, I heard about that, too. Hanging's too good for that one, I tell you. Well, fine." Santos looked around the stable for the first time. "None of these?"

Jacob hesitated. "I was hoping to be able to invest in a more reliable animal."

Santos nodded. "I see." He glared at Caleb. "Well, in that case, just leave it to me. I'll find a mount for you by tomorrow. You can't get the thing killed, though."

"I'll do my best," Jacob said with a grin. "You have any idea why the sheriff down in Jasper can't get his man?"

Santos sighed. "Like I said—Daly managed to get a job working at the Vernon Copper Mine and has apparently made himself indispensable. The boss always has some excuse why he can't be bothered or why they can't reveal his whereabouts."

"All right." Jacob considered what kind of security might be around a mine. "We'll find a way to get to him."

"Damn right, we will," Santos said vehemently. "Glad you'll be joining me, Payne. Come on over to my office. We got a lot to do."

He led the way out of the livery.

"So you won't be taking Smoke?" Caleb asked before Jacob left.

The bounty hunter looked at the other man, exasperated. "The horse that almost *bit* me? No, Caleb. Not this time."

Caleb nodded, while Jacob hurried to catch up with Santos and prepare to track down the outlaw Daly.

CHAPTER TWO

The ride south to Jasper took two full days, the marshal cursing the town's sheriff the whole time. The horse Santos had rounded up for Jacob before they left Tucson was sufficient, though nothing to get all that excited about.

"His name is Yellow," Santos had said when he met Jacob outside his hotel at dawn. "He belongs to my neighbor. I told him we'd be back within the week."

Jacob approached Yellow, letting the animal smell him before he climbed on. "Hey there, boy."

He pet the animal's long neck and shoulder. The horse was a deep chestnut brown with white stockings on its two front feet. It was alert and gentle. But one thing it was not was yellow.

"Yellow, huh? Please tell me he's not called that on account of his lack of courage."

Santos laughed. "I couldn't say. I guess we'll find out."

Jacob grinned. At least the animal didn't bite.

"Okay, Yellow. You and me, huh?" The horse nuzzled his ear. "Yeah, I think we'll get along just fine, Marshal."

"Glad to hear it, seeing as we don't have any other options. Let's get moving. I'd like to get as far as we can before dark."

Now, more than thirty hours later, Jacob and Yellow followed closely behind Santos and his horse as they crossed over into the outskirts of Jasper.

This was Jacob's first visit to the town, but Santos had filled him in on the history. The town had been built up around the Vernon Copper Mine, which was run by the Rockville Mining Company. When copper was discovered there three years ago, the Vernon brothers had bought up all the claims and monopolized the area. Jasper—named after one of the brothers—was a company town, almost entirely populated by miners, with the occasional soiled dove, bartender, preacher, and a handful of other industrious business people who saw a chance to make money.

They approached Jasper from the north, through the low hills full of scrub and cactus. The first buildings they came to were seemingly abandoned boarding houses, far from the town center. Whoever lived there, likely bachelor miners, were gone for the day. Every block or so, they'd tip their hats to the women hanging clothes out to dry, hauling water, or weeding in the small dirt yards around the clapboard houses.

The street Santos led them through wound downhill, through the small residential area, until Jacob began to recognize what must be the main street of Jasper. He counted no fewer than three separate saloons within a four-block stretch and chuckled to himself. Maybe that's one of the reasons the sheriff here was having so much trouble.

"Are we going straight to the mine?" Jacob asked.

Santos reined his horse to let Jacob catch up with him. "Not just yet. It's far to the south of town. I figure we'll stop by the jail and see if the sheriff has any news for us. If not, we can get us settled in a hotel and make our assault on the mine tomorrow."

"Assault?" Jacob grinned. "You got it, boss."

"That's right—assault. Seeing as whatever pleading and reasoning Sheriff Alway has tried ain't working, that's probably the next step. If words don't work, I have no problem using my gun. Which is why I brought along my temporary deputy."

Jacob's grin widened. "Glad to be of service."

Before they began to move again, Jacob heard a plaintive voice coming from farther down the road.

"Come on, Oscar. I don't want to have to shoot you."

Santos and Jacob exchanged a quick glance before nudging their horses ahead to wherever this Oscar person was. They turned the next right corner to find a portly man, who could only be the sheriff with that gleaming badge, yanking on the arm of another man who was clearly passed out drunk in the dusty road. Even from this distance, Jacob could tell the drunk was unconscious and not able to even hear the sheriff's commands, let alone follow them.

"Oscar, I done told you and told you. Destroying

Miss Jessie's property is grounds for arrest. You're gonna have to spend the night in the jail, so let's get you there."

He yanked again, the other man's dead weight barely moving a couple inches. The sheriff dropped the limp arm to the ground and fumbled for his gun.

"Sheriff," Santos called, his voice carrying across the distance. "You wouldn't be getting ready to shoot an unarmed, unconscious man, would you?"

Sheriff Alway looked up, surprised. "This man is not defenseless. He just overturned two Faro tables at Jessie's Parlor."

"That may be true, but that was then. Take a look at the man now, Sheriff." Santos dismounted and tossed his reins to Jacob. The bounty hunter watched as the marshal approached the sheriff, his right hand casually but pointedly resting on the grip of his revolver, still in its holster. "How much has this man had to drink?"

"I really couldn't say. I'm sorry, I didn't catch your name."

"I'm U.S. Marshal Owen Santos. You might recall the name, since you wired for me to come down from Tucson to save your sorry ass."

That seemed to have been a magic word. As soon as Santos announced his title, Sheriff Alway grasped his hand, pumping it up and down and all but blubbering in his joy.

"Mr. Santos! Oh, thank goodness. Yes, sir. Just as you say, I'll not be drawing a gun on"—he nudged the man at his feet—"Mr. Tunney. We'll get him nice and comfy in a jail cell where he can sleep it off."

Jacob dismounted and led the horses to where Santos was helping Alway commandeer a couple bystanders to carry the unconscious Tunney. Alway, Santos, Jacob, and their two horses followed behind two men holding up Oscar between them, crossing the street and carrying him into the Jasper jail.

As the two bystanders carried the drunken man inside, the sheriff stayed on the boardwalk and tried to get rid of the marshal and Jacob.

"You see, Mr. Santos, you've caught me at a bad time. It's a real shame I've gotta process this fella now and can't accompany you."

"It's about what we expected, Alway."

"You boys want I should make you a map to the mine office? Mr. Farnsworth is usually there all hours of night if you want to talk to him now."

"I think it's better if we head down to the mine first thing tomorrow," Santos said.

"It's getting dark," Jacob said in agreement, looking up at the sky. With Jasper situated between the hills as it was, the sun had already set half an hour earlier. The soft purple sky was quickly turning to black as stars began popping into view. "I don't want to be caught unawares. Tomorrow would be better. Let's find a place to sleep for the night."

"Just as you say. Oscar will keep a bit yet while I see to you. Come along, fellas," Sheriff Alway said. "Let's introduce you to Mrs. Courtland."

As they crossed the threshold into the three-story hotel built into the hill, a curvy blonde crossed the room to greet them, beaming. She wore a deceptively low-cut dress, with a filmy lace covering her decolletage.

"Abby," Sheriff Alway called. Jacob noticed he didn't bother to remove his hat. "I'd like you to take special care of these guests of mine. This here is U.S. Marshal Santos from Tucson, and his deputy Mr. Payne."

Jacob doffed his hat, bowing his head slightly as he took Mrs. Courtland's offered hand.

"Abby Courtland," she said with a dazzling, dimpled smile. As she bobbed her head, several curls fell forward into her face. She giggled, pushing them back with her free hand. "It's always a joy when the sheriff brings me guests."

"Right, well. We're mighty lucky they're here." The sheriff clapped his hand on Santos's shoulder. "I'll let you boys rest a bit and come see about breakfast in the morning. I can't tell you enough how much I appreciate you being here, Marshal."

"Our pleasure, Sheriff. We'll see you in the morning."

"I've got just the place for y'all," Mrs. Courtland said. "Come upstairs with me."

She led the way past a young girl at the foot of the stairs who tried to catch Jacob's eye. When she leaned toward him, he smiled politely but didn't turn his focus from the matter at hand. The second floor of the hotel seemed just as noisy as the saloon on the ground floor, but Mrs. Courtland kept leading them farther up into the third floor. There were fewer rooms up here, with less evidence of heavy traffic.

"No one will bother y'all up here. I hope you get a good chance to rest. Your room rate includes supper and a whiskey downstairs. I believe we're serving stew tonight. I'll go tell Wilbur to look for you," she explained as she led them down the hallway. "Here's Mr. Payne's room."

She opened the room to her right and let the door swing open, stepping back to let Jacob go in first.

"Thank you, ma'am."

She nodded. "There's a wash basin on the dresser, and an extra blanket at the foot of the bed. I'll go get Mr. Santos settled and then come back to check on you," she said, touching his arm lightly.

Once he was left alone, Jacob tossed his bag onto the bed and looked around. The furniture was worn, scratched in some places, but solid. The floral wallpaper looked brand new. He thought about how hard it must be for Mrs. Courtland to run this business by herself, and how pleased she must have been when she had saved enough money to paper the rooms. But then, Jacob had seen many remarkable women in the west, called to do any number of remarkable things they wouldn't have even thought to do if they had stayed in the safe cities in the eastern states. Mrs. Courtland must be one of these.

He had just finished washing his face and hands for supper when he heard a light knock on the door. With a towel still in one hand, he opened the door to find his hostess standing there beaming at him. Something about her smile made Jacob feel like this woman was genuinely happy to see him, and not just pretending to be like she might for other guests.

"How is everything, Mr. Payne? I see you found the towels. Did you see there's a hook here on the back of the door for your hat or coat if you like?"

"Thank you, Mrs. Courtland. That will be mighty helpful."

"Oh, call me Abby," she said, stepping past him into the room.

Jacob opened the door wider, glancing out into the hallway to see if anyone had seen her enter. He wouldn't want to be a reason anyone makes assumptions about her.

"Well, in that case, you can call me Jacob."

She strolled a tight circle around his room, checked the dust on top of the headboard, and returned to stand near the chair at the door. "Jacob." She smiled at him over her shoulder. "Is there anything I can do for you? Any way I can make your stay more comfortable?"

"No, I don't think so. Thank you. I was just going to head down for supper."

"I could have supper brought up to you if you like." She stepped closer to him; the weight of her skirt pressed against his legs and the warmth of her body crowded around him.

"No—" Jacob cleared his throat. "No, thank you, ma'am."

"You know, Jacob . . ." She placed her hand lightly against his arm again. "The sheriff told me to make sure you're well taken care of. You sure I can't offer you some company? Doesn't have to be mine. I've got a real nice selection of girls for you to choose from."

He put his big hand over her delicate one. He liked the feel of her warm touch on his arm, but not enough to take advantage of her. "No, ma'am. I appreciate the offer. I'm sure your . . . selection is mighty fine. But I didn't come to Jasper to enjoy myself. It wouldn't be right if I was too tired tomorrow to assist the marshal."

"Why did y'all come to Jasper?" she asked after a beat. She withdrew her hand and made herself comfortable in the only chair in the room, apparently not offended by his gentle rejection of her offers.

Jacob hesitated. It didn't seem proper to sit on the bed with a lady in the room, but neither did it seem proper to stand over her. He compromised by perching himself uncomfortably on the footboard, praying it would hold under his weight.

"I'm not sure how much I'm allowed to say, ma'am."

"Abby."

"Abby. I'm not really a deputy. This is just a temporary assignment, so I'm not too sure what the rules are."

"I see."

"But, I will say that Marshal Santos and me came down here because your sheriff asked for our help capturing an outlaw."

Her expression hardened. For a fleeting moment, Jacob wondered if he had offended her somehow. And then, through clenched teeth, she said, "You wouldn't be here after Floyd Daly, would you?"

CHAPTER FOUR

Jacob gaped at the woman. "How did you— That is, I'm not supposed to say, but why do you ask about Floyd Daly?"

"Oh!" Abby looked furious. "That man is rotten to the core. He should have been brought to justice long before now. I keep telling the sheriff, but that man couldn't teach a hen to cluck. Nice enough, but *nice* don't cut it when we're dealing with a monster like Daly. I tell you what, Mr. Payne—if it *is* Floyd Daly you come down here to capture, I'll help you in any way I can. And if it's someone else, might I suggest you also look into Daly before you leave town?"

Jacob chuckled. "I might as well tell you it is Daly. I don't think the marshal would like me to be starting up a list of folk that Alway should be taking care of on his own."

"But he hasn't been. Don't you see?" She leaned forward excitedly. "Daly may have already been a wanted man when he arrived in Jasper, but that hasn't stopped him from his despicable behavior here. He's been stealing and cheating nearly every person in this town, and Sheriff should have locked him up long ago."

"Why hasn't he?"

"Scared." She leaned back again. "Mr. Farnsworth at the mine has taken quite a shine to Daly, and Sheriff is petrified of upsetting him. The Rockville Mining Company owns this town—or most of it. Enough that Sheriff probably thinks pleasing Mr. Farnsworth is the way to get reelected."

"It's not?"

Abby shook her head. "I'm not sure, but I don't think so. There are enough business owners besides Farnsworth who want the law working the way it should that any vote would be close."

"Even if there's not, that's no reason for the sheriff to not arrest the criminal. How does Daly keep getting away with it?"

"Too many people in this town work for the mine and want to keep Mr. Farnsworth happy. I don't know why he likes Daly so much, anyway. Any criminal like that is just waiting for a chance to take in another victim. It's just a matter of time before he cheats the mining company the same way he's cheated everyone else in this town."

"I don't doubt you're right."

"If you really can bring in Daly and stop him from taking advantage of every breathin' man, woman, and child, you'll be doing the town of Jasper an enormous service. We all deserve justice same as any other town.

And Sheriff Alway will be reminded of that come the next election."

A knock on Jacob's open door startled them.

"You want to head down for supper?" Santos asked. "Everything okay here? Mrs. Courtland, is my deputy bothering you?"

"Oh no, not at all." She stood and exited into the hallway. "I was just filling him in a little about Jasper and how grateful we are that you boys are here to help Sheriff Alway."

Santos looked at Jacob questioningly.

"Let's go eat. I'll give you the details," Payne muttered.

By the time they reached the saloon downstairs, Santos knew as much about what had been going on in Jasper as Jacob did. Abby found them a seat, then went to get their food.

Once she was out of earshot, Payne said, "I'm not sure an assault first thing tomorrow is the best plan, Marshal."

Abby returned carrying two glasses of whiskey, followed just behind by a girl carrying three bowls of steaming stew.

"You don't mind if I join you, do you, gentlemen?"

"Our pleasure, ma'am," Jacob said as he stood to help Abby into her chair.

"Don't let me interrupt," Abby said as she sat.

Santos nodded. "What were you saying, Payne?"

"I think we should try talking to Mr. Farnsworth first, before we try anything forceful."

"Talking?" Santos shook his head and took a bite

of stew. "From what I hear, all that's been done is talking."

"That may be, but if what our host here says is true, I'm not sure we can trust Sheriff Alway's version of events. Mrs. Courtland—"

"Abby."

"—Abby. You say you know of more Jasper citizens who have been cheated by this Daly?"

She nodded vigorously. "I do. I can think of, oh, five or six right now. And I bet there's more."

"Does Mr. Farnsworth know about these other . . . indiscretions?"

Abby thought for a moment, staring into the space above Jacob's shoulder before answering. "I don't know. Could be he hasn't. I don't know anyone brave enough to tell him."

"Not even you?" Jacob teased.

"Oh, you joke, Jacob Payne, but I would march over there right now in the pitch dark if I thought it would do any good." Her dimples winked at him when she retorted.

"I do not doubt that at all. Won't be necessary, though. Not yet."

"What are you suggesting, Payne?" Santos said.

"From what we've been told, there's been a lot of talk but maybe not by the right people. If Abby can get some of the other Jasper citizens to come with us, to establish a pattern of behavior, maybe Mr. Farnsworth will see that it's in his best interest to turn over Daly to the law now, before he gets swindled himself."

Jacob took a bite of his stew and let Santos think

over his proposal without pushing any further. He didn't know if his plan would work. Probably not, actually. But he hated the idea of bringing violence to the mine, of disturbing the other men's place of work —especially if it could be avoided. There would be time for that if that's what it came to, but maybe they could win over Mr. Farnsworth first.

"All right, Payne. We'll try it your way first. It can't hurt. Abby, can you gather a few of your friends, like you were saying? Meet us here right after breakfast?"

"I'll write them all notes tonight and send them with a couple of my girls. I assure you, gentlemen, Jasper is full of folk who want to see Floyd Daly brought to justice."

"I'm glad to hear it," Santos said, and Payne nodded in agreement. "Tomorrow we'll figure out how to deliver that justice."

CHAPTER FIVE

The next morning, after breakfast, Jacob and Santos walked out of Abby's hotel to find her speaking to a cluster of three men and another woman on the boardwalk. Abby seemed to be in the middle of an animated explanation when they interrupted.

"This them?" Santos asked.

"Yes, sir," Abby said, grandly gesturing. "Each of these fine citizens you see before you has been cheated, robbed, or double-crossed by Floyd Daly."

"And y'all are willing to testify to that?"

They all nodded.

"Yes, sir," the older man said. "I been waiting for a chance to say my piece."

"And you know that we're going to go talk to Mr. Farnsworth of the Rockville Mining Company before we do anything else, don't you?"

The older man frowned, and then looked back at Abby. "Well now, Abby, you didn't say nothing about going to the mine first."

"Well . . ." She fiddled with the ruffle at the end of her sleeve. "I didn't exactly know that's what would be asked of them."

"Hmm," Santos said, frowning. "Gentlemen, ma'am. I appreciate you coming down here first thing this morning. I know you all must be very busy people. But if Mrs. Courtland here wasn't clear, let me tell you that we are planning on taking your accusations to Mr. Farnsworth. We believe—we hope—that showing him that his treasured employee has demonstrated a pattern of untrustworthy behavior will help us capture Daly without too much interruption or bloodshed."

"Oh no, I couldn't," the woman said in a whisper. "My Bill is a foreman at the mine. I couldn't—he could lose his job, and then what would we do?"

"I understand, Missus . . . ?"

"Mrs. Lennox."

"Of course. Mrs. Lennox." Santos took her hand in both of his. "We don't want to ask you to take on any risk you're not comfortable taking. Why don't you head on home today? We'll let you know if we need you to testify for a judge."

"Oh, thank you," she said, still in a whisper. She darted down the street before anyone could ask anything else of her.

"I'm not sure about this either," the older man said.

Santos waved him away without another word and turned his attention to the two remaining men, one holding a bowler hat in his hand and wearing a neat, gray jacket, the other glaring at Jacob as though he were to blame for the fact that the man was awake so early.

"And you two?" Jacob asked them.

Bowler Hat offered his hand to both lawmen to shake. "I'm Arthur Devlin. I run the general store just up the ways there." He indicated with his thumb, pointing up the street. "I'm not afraid of the mine officials. They need me to keep the wives happy with their ribbons and other doodads. Daly has run up a hell of a bill with me, and now he just laughs it off when I press him about it."

"Thank you, Mr. Devlin. I appreciate you being willing to share your experience." Jacob turned to the final man, eyebrows raised.

The glaring man spat in the dirt next to him. "Daly cheats at cards," he declared.

Santos and Jacob exchanged a look. That news seemed unsurprising.

"I'm sorry to hear that, Mister—" Jacob began.

"Sorry, nothin'." He spat again. "They call me Gentle Jack. I'm the only Gentle Jack in Jasper, and Daly'll know. He knows. He bilked me out of all of last month's pay. The man cheats."

"So this was recent?" Jacob clarified.

Gentle Jack nodded. "This last time, yeah."

"He's done this before?"

"Course he has. 'Bout every few weeks or so I fancy a game. This last time was the worst, though."

"All right," Santos said, clapping a hand on both men's shoulders. "If you two can gather your horses, my deputy and I will lead the way. We'll be able to meet with Mr. Farnsworth and bring our concerns to his attention."

"Think we should wait for the sheriff?" Jacob asked.

Santos frowned. "I doubt it. He's probably at home right now coming up with his excuses to stay in."

"Abby, will you be joining us?" Jacob asked.

"I sure will. Wilbur knows he's in charge till I get back. I can't wait to get my hands on Daly."

Jacob laughed. "How about you leave that to us?"

"We'll see," she replied darkly.

The road to the mining office was wide and well traveled. What it lacked in shade it made up for in direct, level traveling path, much different from the winding, hilly road they had entered town on.

After about a half an hour's ride, Gentle Jack pointed out a low building in the distance that looked like it was being held together with chicken wire. Jacob was pleased to see the mining official at least had no vanity or pretension in his place of business.

"That there is the offices of Rockville Mining Company," Jack said.

"And Mr. Farnsworth should be there?" Santos asked.

"As far as I've heard, he never leaves," Abby quipped.

Jacob didn't join in the conversation, keeping his attention fixed on the office building and the workers milling around it. As they got closer, he noticed that while most of the workers were going in and out of the office or working on construction nearby, there was one shadowy figure that stood around the corner of the building seemingly doing nothing. Jacob suspected that man was watching him as closely as he himself was being watched.

Jacob unhooked his hammer loop. He sat up straighter in his saddle, letting his full height and breadth be seen. Not many men would tussle willingly with Jacob Payne.

Santos led the caravan of horses to the mining office, hitching his mount to the post outside. He moved to help Abby off hers, but she had already reached the ground and waved away his offered hand.

"Mr. Santos, the only thing I need help with will be keeping my temper."

She smiled at him to show she was joking, but Jacob caught the look in her eye. He would try to stay between Abby and Daly if need be.

Jacob hung back, watching for signs of Daly as the others all filed into the office. The shadowy figure, a small man with a black, wide-brimmed hat pulled over his eyes, still lurked by the corner of the building. The bounty hunter wasn't able to get a good look at him before he ducked back, but he had his suspicions. He didn't like letting that man out of his sight, but Santos needed Jacob inside.

He opened the door and stepped into the cool, dark office.

CHAPTER SIX

The Rockville Mining Company office at the Vernon Copper Mine in Jasper, Arizona, consisted of one single large room, divided in half by a partial wall, partitioning Mr. Farnsworth's office from that of his secretary. Jacob hung back near the door to take it all in. The building had just the single door, with a window on either side. None of the other three walls offered any way in or out of the room—which could be good or bad, depending on the situation. Jacob eyed the secretary's desk in front of him, trying to discern if it had any hidden compartments for weapons or other defensive mechanisms.

Mr. Farnsworth may trust Floyd Daly, but that didn't mean Jacob shouldn't be prepared for the day Daly might turn on him.

Santos had introduced himself and his party to the secretary, a serious young man who had already found a way to mention in conversation that he had attended Harvard University. Even though Mr.

Farnsworth could clearly hear the entire conversation and was sitting only ten feet away, the secretary behaved as though his boss were in a high tower somewhere else.

"I'm afraid I can't let you speak to Mr. Farnsworth without an appointment."

Santos pulled out his U.S. Marshal badge. "I believe the law always has a standing appointment, young man."

"Humphries, it's fine," Farnsworth grunted from the back of the room. "Send them back. I don't want you to waste more time arguing about it."

Humphries frowned and gestured for the group to cross into the older man's office. Farnsworth stood behind his desk to greet them. He held his pocket watch in hand and glanced at it over and over in between watching the visitors enter.

"I'll give you five minutes," he said, still standing.

"I appreciate you taking the time, Mr. Farnsworth," Santos began.

"Get on with it," the mining official said.

"I understand you have a man in your employment by the name of Floyd Daly."

"This again?" Farnsworth plopped into his chair and put his feet on his desk. "I already told Sheriff Alway that he has the wrong man. Floyd Daly must be a very popular name. There's no way my man is the thief and murderer Alway has described."

"I think we can clear that up pretty easily, Mr. Farnsworth," Jacob said. "As U.S. Marshal, Mr. Santos has the wanted poster asking for Floyd Daly's arrest, which of course includes an illustration which might help clear up your confusion. I'm surprised Sheriff Alway didn't show you his copy of it."

"Oh, he tried to, at first. But I don't believe it. Mr. Daly has increased production here by nearly three hundred percent."

He paused to let that number sink in. Jacob didn't want to think about what Daly had done or threatened to do in order to get that number.

"That may be, Mr. Farnsworth," Jacob said. "But we have reason to believe your employee has a demonstrated pattern of behavior that indicates he will steal from the company or cheat you directly. We'd like to take him into custody before that happens—if it hasn't already."

"Oh, you say you're looking out for me, do you? I don't believe it. I don't want to hear it." Farnsworth looked up from his pocket watch and frowned at the crowd that had invaded his office. "I believe your five minutes is up."

"Mr. Farnsworth." Abby stepped out from the group of men and fluttered her eyelashes at the mining executive. Jacob noticed that she had banished all sounds of anger or frustration from her voice. "You must be a very smart man to have hired such a productive new employee. Especially seeing as he probably doesn't even have mining experience."

He eyed her warily. "Yes, I think so . . ."

"I am a business woman myself," she said, placing a delicate hand to her bosom. "I try to make as smart of hires as I can, and I certainly am always careful to keep my best employees happy."

"What kind of business do you run, miss?"

"But at the same time," she continued, ignoring his question, "I understand that I cannot possibly know every little thing that goes on in my business. That's when I'm grateful to get other people's opinions."

Mr. Farnsworth exhaled a groan.

"For example, Mr. Devlin here." She gestured to the neatly dressed man standing on her left. "He has had many interactions with Floyd Daly, and each of them has left him poorer than the last."

After a moment of silence, she elbowed Devlin in the side, prodding him forward.

"Ahem." He cleared his throat. "That's right. Mr. Daly was a customer of mine since he moved to Jasper, but—"

"But can you really call him a *customer*," Abby interrupted, "if he has never paid his bills?"

"That's right." Devlin nodded, Abby's confidence seeming to bolster his own. "Mr. Daly opened a credit account at my store—using his job at your own company as collateral, Mr. Farnsworth. But he has yet to pay a single dime of what he owes me."

"You want me to pay his bills, is that it?" Farnsworth asked, pulling out his money clip. He peeled a bill off the top and tossed it across the desk.

The bill floated to the ground at Devlin's feet. He looked confused, but bent to pick it up. "No, I—"

"He owes *me* money, too," Gentle Jack shouted.

"Mr. Farnsworth, we seem to have lost the thread here." Santos spoke soothingly, trying to regain control of the conversation. "These fine citizens are all here to testify about how they have been wronged by the man currently in your employ. If you could tell us where to find him, so that we may apprehend him in accordance with the law, we hope to stop him from wronging you or your company."

Farnsworth stood again, this time coming around his desk. Jacob hoped for a short moment that they had gotten through to him, despite what his gut was telling him.

"Your five minutes was up long ago, and I have been more than polite. The only ones costing me or Rockville Mining Company money are you lot, so I'll see you out. Good day."

Even with five people in their group, unless Santos indicated they should get violent and physical with Mr. Farnsworth, there was nothing they could do. Without Daly anywhere in the room, there was no call for the law to do anything other than leave the company in peace.

Jacob waited to exit last, still looking for that one hint that would indicate that Farnsworth and Humphries were ready for whatever might befall them, but the solid walls of wooden planks looked bare.

CHAPTER SEVEN

"Now what do we do?" Abby demanded as they stepped out of the mining office.

Devlin still held the twenty-dollar bill loosely in his hand. Abby snatched it from him.

"We are all owed money," she said, before he could object. "If this is all we're getting, we'll have to split it."

"He owes me money, too," Gentle Jack said—again practically shouting the words.

Santos tried to calm them down, but Abby and Jack were already yelling at each other.

Jacob inched around to the side of the building where he had seen the man watching them earlier. None of the other workers came over to this corner; it was farthest away from the mine and the water supply, and there were no entrances to the office on that side.

The bounty hunter approached cautiously, his hand on his grip.

The shade of a nearby tree hit this side of the building, creating a curtain of dappled shadow that made it difficult for Jacob to immediately identify any footprints or other possible clues. He stopped to listen, but the bustling and arguing of the group behind him was too distracting. He sniffed, checking to see if he could smell an unwashed outlaw, but no aroma stood out to his keen nose.

Five more steps brought Jacob around the corner of the office, but there was no one skulking around here either, and as far as he could see, there were no clues or indications of where the man had gone.

It had to have been Daly, though. Jacob could not think of any other reason a man would sneak around watching a U.S. Marshal and his deputy unless that man was a wanted outlaw. All this meant Daly was likely somewhere nearby. He wasn't in the office, nor was he around the office anymore.

Jacob turned around and strode off to the mouth of the Vernon Copper Mine.

This early in the day, there were only a handful of cars full of ore above ground. Men covered in a thin coat of dirt, hats pulled low over their eyes pushed past Jacob to go down into the shaft. He hesitated; confronting and trying to capture the outlaw in the dark mine could put all of these other workers at risk. He eyed each man he passed, trying to see if one of them might be Daly.

If a man wanted to hide, the deep, dark reaches of a mine might be a good place to do it. Jacob was sure that he'd find the man in this pit if he looked hard enough.

He ignored the questioning looks a few of the miners shot at him. There was no time to explain. Daly could already be deep in the recesses. Jacob crossed into the mouth of the hole, pausing only a moment to let his eyes adjust to the darkness. The banging, tumbling rock, and shouting orders were louder in here. He couldn't cease all production, so he'd just have to do a visual search. In the dark.

Jacob took a deep breath and began his descent.

Twenty yards into the mine, a mancart stood waiting to ferry workers farther down. Jacob briefly tried to explain to the man in charge what he was doing here, but the worker didn't seem to care. He just ushered Jacob into the cart with the other men and transferred him down to the next level. Once farther below, the workers scattered, leaving Jacob to wonder which way to go.

Before the last of the miners disappeared into the darkness out of his sight, Jacob stopped him, grabbing his arm.

"Where can I find Daly?"

"Shoot, I don't know, mister."

"Guess."

"I'm not sure I should."

"I've got a deputy U.S. Marshal badge that says you should."

"All right, all right." The miner shook off Jacob's grip. "No need to threaten. Daly could be anywhere, really. He seems to have a finger in every pie."

"But if you had to pick?" Jacob was getting impatient.

"If I had to pick . . . well, lately Daly's been

spending more time in the older shafts. Down that way." He pointed to the shaft behind Jacob and to the left. "There aren't many still working that shaft, though. You'd better take a candle with you."

"Thanks."

"Be careful. That flame burns too much, you're liable to lose your breath."

"I got it."

Jacob grabbed one of the last candles that rested on a table at the foot of the cart track and lit it, holding it carefully in front of him. Anyone who came down later would just be out of luck.

As he started down the shaft the miner had indicated, Jacob unholstered his revolver. He would prefer to take Daly without any bloodshed, but he knew that wasn't always possible. He held the candle up in front of him. The flickering light, combined with the rock walls around him, cast harsh shadows. Twice Jacob went to turn down another branch of tunnel only to find out it was simply a depression in the wall, filled with darkness.

After thirty yards of cautious progress, Jacob still had not run into any other workers. This really was an abandoned shaft of the Vernon Copper Mine. If he did come across Daly down here, and things went south, who knew how long it would be before anyone else came down here.

Jacob thought he heard some kind of shuffling. It could be a rat, bat, or other creature, but he paused to listen more carefully. Somewhere near him—maybe just around that next turn in the tunnel—was *something*.

Something alive. Something moving.

He took another few steps toward the sound. He held his breath, not wanting to give anything away. Now he was almost sure those were footsteps. It sounded like heavy boots on the mine's rock floor.

He took another three steps, just reaching the turn in the tunnel.

A swift breath blew out his candle flame.

In the darkness, Jacob heard the click of a hammer being pulled back.

He inched toward the sound, but before he could relight his candle, the crack of gunshot echoed through the chamber.

The dirt wall behind Jacob exploded where the bullet hit, just inches to his left but fortunately missing him. The shot had been fired from relatively close by—his ears rang from the blast. The ringing began to fade, and the first noise Jacob could identify was footsteps running deeper into the mine, away from him.

That was too close. And if Jacob had been shot, he would never have made it out of here. Trying to capture Daly while inside the mine was too big of a risk. Jacob kicked the rock wall in frustration and made his way back up to the surface, leaving Daly to his dark hidey-hole.

As he returned to the daylight, Jacob did his best to avoid running into any miners. He had been deep underground, but that didn't mean the sound of a gunshot had gone unnoticed.

When he emerged back into the light, he noticed Santos and the group still waiting for him. The marshal sat atop his horse, eyes scanning the horizon in all directions. When his gaze fell on Jacob, the other man's shoulders visibly relaxed.

"Payne!"

He dismounted and hurried over to where Jacob was exiting the mine. As he got closer, Jacob realized how much he must have worried Santos. The man was frowning and reaching out to grab Jacob as soon as he was close enough.

"What happened? Where did you go? I thought I heard a gunshot, but I wasn't sure. I don't like the idea of us splitting up." Santos began brushing dirt off Jacob's sleeve. He hadn't realized how much the exploding wall had hit him in the dark.

"He almost shot me," Jacob said. "In the dark. Daly shot at me. I didn't even know he was there. We've got to come up with a better plan."

Santos nodded soberly. "Let's head back to Jasper and reassess."

Jacob started toward the horses, but the marshal stopped him.

"It'll be easier to do this once we no longer have the whole gang with us," Santos said in a whisper.

Jacob nodded and made his way to where Yellow stood, patiently waiting for him.

"You okay?" Abby asked cautiously.

"Fit as a fiddle," he said. "The man surprised me in the dark, but it takes more than a shock to take down Jacob Payne."

Abby laughed at his bravado. "All right, Mr. Payne. Just don't you go dying on me before we get justice, ya hear?"

"Wouldn't think of it." He climbed on his horse,

taking the reins from the miner who had untied Yellow for him.

"We all ready?" Santos asked the group.

Among a chorus of yeses, the marshal led them back up the road to town. He rode ahead, listening to Gentle Jack rant and rave angrily about all the injustices done him. Jacob didn't hear everything he said, but caught the general idea. He was happy to trail in the back of the group, making sure no one got separated but also able to have a private conversation with Abby.

"How long have you lived in Jasper?" he asked her.

She smiled and flashed a dimple at him. "Why? You thinking about staying around?"

He chuckled. "No, nothing like that. Just wondering what brought you here."

Her smile grew strained, but she didn't give any other indication she was distressed by his question. All she said was, "I came here a couple years ago. From South Carolina."

"Really? I thought I heard some southern in that accent of yours."

"Yes, sir. After the war a lot of things changed in our hometown, so we lit on out of there to look for a new chance somewhere else."

Jacob almost didn't want to ask the next question, didn't want to seem like he was prying. But he asked anyway. "We?"

They rode in silence for a minute or two. Jacob wasn't even sure she had heard his question until she looked at him again. She didn't say a word, but just from her set jaw and pained expression he could tell his question had struck a nerve.

"How exactly were you cheated by Floyd Daly?" Jacob asked quietly.

The look she shot him broke his heart. She was trying to be so strong and so brave, but he could tell that Daly had really hurt her. She bit her lip, as though thinking, but they were already to her hotel. Abby dismounted and handed her horse's reins over to her stable boy, who had been waiting for her. She went inside, not say anything more to Jacob.

CHAPTER NINE

Abby's stable boy offered to take care of Jacob's and Santos's horses as well, and Jacob gratefully handed over his reins. He wanted to hurry inside to finish his conversation. What had happened to this poor woman to make her so angry? How exactly had Floyd Daly hurt her?

When he stepped inside, Jacob looked everywhere before finally noticing Abby sitting alone in the corner of her saloon. It was just about lunchtime, but since most of the men in Jasper worked at the mine, business was slow. The room was quiet.

Santos noticed Abby about the same time and elbowed Jacob forward.

"You go," he said in a low tone. "I'll get us food. I get the feeling she doesn't want to be crowded."

Jacob nodded, removing his hat and crossing the room. As he reached Abby's table, one of her waitresses brought a glass of beer and set it down in front of her.

"Can I get you one, Mr. Payne?"

"Coffee?"

The waitress nodded and left.

"You not drinking with me, Jacob?" Abby smiled at him, but he could tell her heart wasn't in her teasing.

He reached across the table and put his hand over hers. "What happened, Abby?"

She withdrew her hand from his and scooted her chair away—only a couple inches, but enough for him to notice. She kept her eyes on him while she gulped back several large swallows of beer. He returned his hands to his lap and waited. She would tell him when she was ready, or she would leave. He didn't want to force her.

The waitress returned with his coffee. He thanked her, and once she left again Jacob and Abby sat in silence for nearly a minute. Jacob was debating whether or not to get up and leave her alone when she finally spoke.

"I haven't told you how I came by this place, have I?"

"No, ma'am."

She nodded and drained her beer before speaking again.

"I came out west with my husband and his brother two years ago. My husband had been diagnosed with consumption, and the doctor told us the dry air in the west would be the best treatment. My brother-in-law had a hankering for space and a change, so he came with us."

Jacob couldn't see where this was leading, or what

this had to do with Floyd Daly, but he stayed quiet, sipping his coffee as he listened.

"It's a good thing he did come with us, since my husband—his name was Jacob, too, if you'll believe it—he died while we were still in Texas. He never even made it to Arizona. Joseph and me stayed to bury him, and I suppose I could have gone back to South Carolina, but I wanted to see it all the way to the end. So Joseph and me kept on till we landed here in Jasper. Two years ago, like I said.

"It was hard when we first got here. Joseph tried out mining and I kept house, and we went on like that for a few months. But . . ."

She trailed off and looked out toward the window. An older man driving a cart proceeded down the road. Jacob took the moment of Abby's distraction as a chance to glance behind him. Santos was leaning on the bar, watching them from a distance.

"Joseph had an accident in the mine," Abby began, and Jacob turned his attention back to her. "I still don't know how it happened, but one of his legs was crushed. Doc Jewett amputated it in time to save his life, but he couldn't work there anymore. We were . . . there never was anything between Joseph and me. He was like my brother, above anything. But still. I couldn't leave him. He was my family, and we were stuck out here in the hills of Arizona with no job, no way to take care of ourselves."

Her eyes had glazed over while she spoke. Jacob was silent.

"Bad luck following bad luck, it was . . . but I guess God done thought we'd had enough. This here hotel came up for sale, and the owner knew we had little else to do and sold it to us for a deal. His wife had died, and I had filled in as cook and maid a couple times for him, and he wanted to go back east. So I gave him everything. All our savings, all my jewelry—my husband's gun, even. That gun had made me feel safe for a year since he'd died, but it was worth trading for a chance at having a real life."

"So it seems like you've done well for yourself," Jacob ventured.

Abby finally met his eyes.

"Right about the time that the hotel was turned over to Joseph and me, Floyd Daly showed up in town."

"Oh."

"I didn't pay him no mind, at first. He even paid his bill for the two weeks he stayed here as a hotel guest. I didn't have any hint of what he was capable of. At first."

She sighed and took another swallow of beer.

"But then, I started to notice Joseph was more and more agitated. He would yell at me for the smallest thing, like throwing away a batch of biscuits that hadn't turned out right, or when I bought more soap than he thought we needed. I couldn't understand why he was so stressed. The hotel was doing good business, so far as I knew. But then one night, Joseph finally cracked under all that pressure. He told me he'd had to borrow money to pay for a share in another mine some fellas were trying to open, and for the new wallpaper upstairs we'd installed recently. He told me this Daly guy had promised to be understanding and would set a reasonable interest, but that he hadn't been able to pay him back fast enough."

Abby paused, letting that sink in.

"I asked him, 'What do we owe?' But he couldn't—he wouldn't—say. Joseph Courtland—this man who had been my brother in all but blood, who I had loved dearly for years—had gone behind my back and . . ."

She buried her face in her hands, elbows leaning on the table. Jacob was shocked. This woman sitting before him had shown such strength and poise; he never would have guessed she was suffering so much.

"Joseph had promised Daly he could have *me*," she whispered into her hands. "I didn't want to agree to it. I threw things and hit Joseph until I had no more strength in me, but it didn't do any good. He just took all of it, because he knew there was no other option. If I didn't go along with the plan, Daly could take the hotel from us. It wasn't until after that awful night that I learned what Joseph had traded me for."

"What?" Jacob asked quietly.

She looked up at him with a wry smile, her eyes rimmed red. "A month's extension. Not in exchange for the money that was owed, or even a portion of the money. No, all Joseph deemed my virtue to be worth was a few extra weeks to come up with the money."

She released a sad, choking laugh.

"Joseph died before that month was even up. I guess he had been hiding his own consumption diagnosis for awhile." She shook her head, amazed. "He's lucky he did, or I might have killed him myself. His life insurance paid off Daly, and I've made my choices in the months since. I take in the girls who have been in my situation, and I help them take care of themselves when no one else will. But that devil won't ever let me forget what he held over us. Over me. He's constantly needling me, offering to pay more for 'another go.' "

"Abby . . ." Jacob risked it again: he cautiously reached across the table to take her hand, and this time she didn't withdraw. Angry tears sprung from her eyes. Tears he wished he could brush away. "We *will* get Floyd Daly. I promise you that. At the very least, he will be behind bars. And I will do everything in my power to make sure you are compensated for what he has cheated you out of, if such a thing can be compensated."

She nodded, but before she could respond, the door banged open and a dirt-covered miner burst into the saloon.

"He's done it," the man gasped out, leaning against the doorframe. "Daly. He's attacked."

Santos was on the man in a second. Jacob rushed to his side, almost upsetting a chair on his way. He looked back at Abby, but she waved him on. In the moment of crisis, her tough, invulnerable exterior had returned.

"Who has he attacked? What's going on?" Santos demanded.

The miner caught his breath. "Daly snapped. I don't know why. I didn't see it. They sent me here to get you."

"All right. We're going."

Jacob ran out the door of the hotel and down the street to the next block, where their horses were just getting brushed down in the livery. He shouted out commands, saddling as he went, and was able to get their horses out and ready in record time. He leapt onto Yellow and led Santos's horse back to the hotel.

In the few minutes he had been gone, the marshal

had managed to dig more details out of the messenger from the mining company.

"Seems there was an explosion down in the mine and while everyone was looking that way, Daly used the distraction to take control of the mining office."

"That bastard," Jacob said.

"We'll get him," Santos assured him. "Abby!" The hotel proprietress was in the doorway, watching them get ready to leave. "Send word to Sheriff Alway, will you? Tell him I want him on the scene."

"You think he'll go?"

"I trust you can make the situation clear to him," he said with a smile.

She nodded, and that was the last thing they saw before they galloped down the road back toward the mine. Moving this fast, their approach took less time than earlier in the morning. The scene at the mine was still chaos, with injured men being carried out of the mineshaft and another crowd of armed men gathering around the office.

"Where is he?" Jacob demanded as they approached.

Two of the workers came forward to take charge of their horses while three others gathered around, all talking at once and relaying the events of the last hour.

"No one saw him go in," the first one said.

"We still don't know how the explosion happened," said the second.

"It was Daly," the third replied. Jacob recognized him as the man who had given him directions in the mine earlier. "I done told you Daly's rotten—*he* set the blast!"

"Okay, fellas, calm down," Santos said in his low, soothing tone. "What matters most is we make sure everyone is safe now. Where is Daly?"

All three men pointed to the office building. Now that they were closer, Jacob noticed that both of the front windows looked to have big wooden boards behind them. There was no clear line of sight into the office.

"Those look like the bookshelves, pushed in front of the window," Santos said. "He's barricaded himself in there. We'll have to figure out how to draw him out."

"We don't know yet what kind of weapons the man has," Jacob said. "Maybe we can find Humphries. He must have known the man."

The sound of horses drew Jacob's attention. Coming down the road, leading a group of half a dozen others, came Abby Courtland. She looked determined. When they got close enough, Jacob noticed that she had another horse tied to her own and was guiding it along with her.

Riding the ponying horse was Sheriff Alway.

Jacob almost laughed at the pained expression on the man's face, but shook his head instead. The man was supposed to be the law in this town. He was the one should be bringing justice to Jasper, Arizona.

Also following Abby were Gentle Jack, Mr. Devlin, and five other townspeople she had somehow managed to gather for the event. Whatever Santos needed to defuse this situation, they had plenty of help on their side.

"Let me talk to Mr. Farnsworth," Santos said. "I need to find out what all is in that office that could be used as a weapon."

Jacob's mind went to those desk drawers he never got to check.

"You can't," the miner said. "Farnsworth is in there. Humphries, too. Daly has taken them hostage."

Santos looked stricken. They already knew Daly was a man who would sacrifice other people for his own gain. Looked like their warning to Farnsworth had come to pass.

"Hostage?" Jacob asked. "What is he demanding?"

The miner shook his head. "Money. Lots of money."

"Damn," Santos cursed under his breath.

"I've got an idea," Jacob said. "You just keep his focus on you."

Santos seemed to catch on quick. "If we can keep him talking, he won't have time to shoot anyone."

"I'm going to find another way in," Jacob said.

The marshal nodded and turned his full body to the office building.

"Come out of there, Daly!" Santos yelled. "This won't end well for you!"

Jacob left Santos shouting at the Rockville Mining Company office and ducked around the corner of the building, where he'd spotted Daly at their first visit to the office. One benefit of Daly having pushed the bookshelves up against the front windows was he wouldn't be able to see where Jacob had gone.

The bounty hunter wondered what the outlaw was doing in there. Robbing Farnsworth? Robbing the entire company? Jacob had noticed the safe in the corner of Farnsworth's office. It was possible it held the pay for the hundreds of men who worked there. A nice haul for a man like Daly.

He stood close to the building and heard a low thrum of talking from inside. The walls were thin—just a handful of pine boards nailed to the frame. He couldn't hear what was said, but there was little enough between Jacob and the men on the other side of the wall that he knew when they were speaking and even where they were standing.

There must be some way he could use that knowledge to his advantage.

Jacob stayed close to the wall, listening, stepping gently so they couldn't hear him too. If Daly was smart, he'd be worried about the fact that he had no line of vision out of the office. But from all the stories Jacob hard heard so far that day, it sounded more like Daly was impulsive than careful. It could have been anything that led him to break his calm facade today rather than any other day.

As he made his way around the back of the office, Jacob realized this was nearest to where Daly must be standing. His voice was noticeably higher than either Farnsworth's or Humphries's, and that voice was louder through the thin wall in the back.

As he watched, the wall itself bowed out a little toward him. He paused, stepping back and watching. His best guess was that Daly, or one of the others, must be leaning against the wall there. The office had been thrown up in a hurry and didn't have the structural strength to hold a grown man's weight. After a minute, Daly must have stood up again because the wall went straight. Jacob crept up to take a closer look.

The corner, where the end of the plank connected to the frame, was ever so slightly coming loose. Not more than a quarter of an inch, but the nails were not holding. If Daly were to lean on the wall again, the board and maybe even the entire wall would come apart.

This was the in Jacob had been waiting for.

He pulled his Bowie knife out of his boot and

carefully inserted the sharp point into the gap by the nail. He would have to go slowly and quietly, so as to not draw Daly's attention. The outlaw would be holding at least one weapon, maybe more, and if Daly thought there was a possible threat on the other side of this wall, he wouldn't hesitate to shoot.

The bounty hunter maneuvered his knife deeper into the gap. He had chosen a spot between the two nails and would soon have the knife far enough in the gap to leverage and widen it.

Just before he was about to tilt his knife up and pry off the board, the weight again fell against the wall. Jacob jumped back and around the corner, letting go of his knife. With Daly's weight again against the wall, the nails fell out even more, pushing the gap in the wall to half an inch.

Jacob could see light through the gap. It was wide enough that he could see the color of the shirt Daly was wearing. Which meant, if the outlaw thought to look, he would be able to see Jacob outside. Jacob held his breath, waiting for him to walk away again.

"That marshal is stupid." The voice Jacob heard didn't sound like Farnsworth or Humphries. He heard the *thud* of something hit the floor near where he stood, maybe the butt of a rifle or shotgun. "He thinks he can just *talk* me into giving myself up?"

Jacob was incensed. Not only was this outlaw a bully, thief, and manipulator, but he had the gall to insult the law as well. He would take great pleasure in bringing this man down.

Daly stood up again and his footsteps on the wooden floorboards told Jacob when he was six feet and then ten feet away. He hurriedly picked up his knife from the ground and again set to work prying the board free of its frame.

He left the board where it was and pulled out the nails on the end closest to him. It balanced precariously, sitting on top of the plank below it. Jacob pulled the board away from the frame to peek inside.

What he saw infuriated him.

Directly across the room from Jacob, Farnsworth and Humphries sat in two small chairs. Daly hadn't even bothered to tie them up, so sure was he that his gun would keep them in line. But, seeing as neither of the other men had weapons or any means of defense, it seemed to have been a pretty good gamble.

Farnsworth caught his glance and widened his eyes. Jacob shook his head, silently pleading with the other man to be quiet. He seemed to know what was needed and called to Daly, drawing attention to himself.

"How else are you gonna get the money you asked for, then, if you don't go out there?"

"I dunno," the outlaw said sullenly. "They'll bring it in here."

"You sure that's all you want, Daly? Just money to get out of town? Seems a bit amateur for a man like you."

"Shut up, old man. You don't know what you're talking about."

"I know there are some people in this town you have pissed off mightily. They're probably all out there right now." Farnsworth pointed at the door. "How're you planning on getting through that crowd."

Throughout this conversation, Jacob pried off the board as quickly and quietly as possible. Farnsworth did a good job of not looking at him over Daly's shoulder, and of keeping his voice raised to disguise any sounds Jacob might be making. Directing his attention to the front of the office was good thinking on his part.

Humphries kept looking at Jacob, but fortunately Daly wasn't paying any attention to him.

"They'll be through that front door any minute," Farnsworth said. "You'd better have a plan."

"They'll not take me," Daly said. He lifted his shotgun up halfheartedly as he backed up toward the corner where Jacob peered in. "I'll see any man come through that door and blast his head off."

"So you think you're going to shoot your way out?" Farnsworth said.

"You got a better idea?" Daly shot back. He slowly moved to lean back against the wall again, near Jacob's corner.

The bounty hunter saw his chance.

Jacob held his breath and pushed his revolver through the gap in the boards.

CHAPTER TWELVE

"Stop right there," Jacob said in a menacing tone.

His revolver was jabbed into the ribs of Floyd Daly.

The outlaw tried to turn his head to see who had stopped him.

"What the—"

"I said stop," Jacob commanded.

With his right hand holding his revolver steady, Jacob used his left hand to rip off more of the planks creating the back wall of the office. Farnsworth groaned at the destruction, but didn't protest. In just a few seconds, Jacob had created a gap big enough for him to step through without removing his gun from Daly's side.

This was the first time Jacob had gotten a good look at the man, but even from behind it was clearly Floyd Daly. He matched the description from the wanted poster perfectly—long dirty blond hair, scraggily dirty blond beard, and only a couple inches taller than five feet.

"This is what we're going to do," Jacob said. "I'm going to count to three. You're going to put your shotgun on the desk with the barrel pointed away from the other men. If you move before I say three, you're dead. If you try to shoot that gun, you're dead. If you dare set the shotgun down in any place or any manner other than what I have specifically told you to do, you're dead. Let me hear you say you understand."

There was a tense moment of almost guttural growling from Daly before Jacob heard him say, "I understand."

"All right, then. One . . . two . . . three."

Jacob moved forward with the outlaw the few inches he needed to lean to set the gun down, his revolver never leaving the other man's side.

"Okay, then. Do you have any other weapons I need to know about?"

"No."

"He's lying," Farnsworth said, almost sounding bored by it. "Of course he does."

"Where?" Jacob demanded.

"Meddling whoremonger—" Daly began.

"Where is it?"

Daly shut his mouth, then said, "I have a derringer tucked into the back of my pants."

Even before he finished the sentence, Jacob had fished the small gun out. "Anything else?"

"A Bowie knife in my right boot," he said through clenched teeth.

"Well, what do you know?" said Jacob. "So do I."

He tucked the derringer into his jacket pocket and stooped to pull the knife out of Daly's boot.

"Are we done?" Jacob asked. "I'm sure you can guess what will happen if I find you've been holding anything back."

"We're done," Daly said petulantly.

"Wonderful. Mr. Humphries," Jacob said to the trembling young man. "Would you please go outside and inform the U.S. Marshal that Floyd Daly has been apprehended?"

He nodded vigorously and all but ran to the front door of the office.

"How are you feeling, Mr. Farnsworth?"

The older man had moved from the chair and was seated against the far wall of the office, arms crossed over his chest. "You certain you have that weasel under control?"

"Yes, sir. There's no reason to be afraid."

"I'm not afraid," he boomed. Farnsworth crossed the room in two strides and began rifling through the outlaw's pockets.

"Hey!" Daly protested.

"I'm taking back what's rightfully mine."

"Can we wait on that, do you think, Mr. Farnsworth?" Jacob asked. "Seems there are a lot of people in this town owed money—and apologies—from this man."

Farnsworth didn't pause in his search. "I'm sure there are. And I'm sure there'd be fewer victims in Jasper if I had listened to Sheriff Alway the first time. I aim to make sure each and every one of them are paid what they are owed. But that starts with stripping this devil of every penny he has on him."

Jacob shook his head. He'd have to let the marshal sort this out.

At that thought, the door opened and several men filed in, Humphries leading Santos and Alway into the office.

"Sheriff, can you see to this criminal, please?" Santos asked calmly.

"We'll take him back to Tucson tomorrow?" Jacob asked.

The marshal nodded. "He can wait. I'd rather make the trip in one piece. I trust Mrs. Courtland still has a room for us at her establishment."

"I'm hankering for more of that stew," Jacob said, grinning.

As they passed the filthy and muttering outlaw over to the custody of the quivering sheriff, Jacob kept both weapons up, ready in case Daly tried to make a run for it in the confusion.

Farnsworth seized the sheriff by the shoulder. "Alway! You had better keep that man locked up until these men can take him to Tucson. If I hear even the breath of a rumor that he's been freed or lost, I will see to it that you never work in this town again."

"No, sir, Mr. Farnsworth. I won't, sir."

"And you boys." He addressed Santos and Jacob. "When will you need me to testify? I'll *walk* all the way to Tucson if it means seeing this man hanged."

"I'll send word when I know for sure, Mr. Farnsworth. We're not expecting the circuit judge before next week sometime."

"Next week it is, then. I'm grateful to you both. Mighty grateful." He shook both of their hands. "It's a damn shame, though. That man did get my mine producing more than it has in years. And now I need to rebuild my office on top of it all."

"But, Mr. Farnsworth," Jacob said. "Would you want that mine producing if it meant he was stealing from or threatening your workers?"

The man looked thoughtful, shrugged, and said again, "It's a damn shame."

Abby had snuck through the office door and directed two of the miners to move the bookshelves back away from the windows. Despite her long road to get where she was, Abby had the temperament and skills of a born manager. Now, without the threat of Daly, Jacob had no doubt she'd make her hotel into the finest and busiest in all the Territory of Arizona.

"You don't have to leave, do you, Mr. Payne? You sure you don't want to stay?" Abby said, sauntering over to him. "I think Jasper'll be needing a new candidate for sheriff right soon."

"That's mighty kind of you, Mrs. Courtland."

"Abby. Please."

Jacob grinned. "Abby. I'm sure whoever steps into that role will be much obliged for your advice and support. But it'll be enough for me to stay one more night and have supper with you."

BLOOD ON THE MOUNTAIN

CHAPTER ONE

"Your deal?" Jacob Payne asked as he tossed his cards into the middle of the poker table. This had never been his game, and he was tempted to just get up and leave, but he couldn't resist trying one more time. He, Edwin, and two strangers had been playing for a couple hours already and Jacob was still running just about even. One more hand—just one more, he kept telling himself—could let him walk away with some real cash.

"Yep," Edwin responded, pulling all the cards toward him.

"This is my last hand," Jacob announced.

There was a short lull while Edwin gathered the deck to shuffle, but no sooner had Jacob breathed a sigh of relief that none of the men were ribbing him for being done than one of the strangers, the one with the mustache, brought up his complaint again.

"Look, I'm just sayin' . . . them Mormons should stay with their own kind."

"They're not hurting you," Jacob said for what felt like the fortieth time. "The man and his family have a homestead miles away from here, aren't coming to bother you or preach to you. What under the canopy is the actual problem?"

"It's just not right," the man said. He leaned his chair back on just the rear legs so he could reach the spittoon. His gob of yellowy-brown saliva fell about an inch short and dribbled down the outside of the metal container. "He's got five wives, I heard. And each one of 'em has a passel of kids. It ain't right."

"Now, how does that work, exactly?" Edwin asked with a grin. "Do the wives all sleep in the same bed? Do they have different rooms? Or do they each get their own house and the fella has to move between each one?"

The mustached stranger—Jacob thought his name was Abe—grimaced. "I don't know," he insisted. "It ain't my business."

"Did you even meet the man?" Jacob asked.

Abe was speechless for only a moment before spluttering, "I didn't need to *meet* him to know. I heard. And it's not right."

Jacob sighed. It was impossible to argue with someone who didn't have any actual point. "You about ready for that next hand?" he asked Edwin.

The dealer grinned and nodded.

The other stranger had remained silent this whole time, but at least his aim with tobacco was better. Jacob eyed him surreptitiously as they played. Abe had called the silent one Lucky, but there was no telling if that was the name he always went by or just one of several different aliases.

As a bounty hunter, Jacob had to keep his suspicions always at the forefront, not taking anything at face value, as though sinister possibilities were everywhere. Because in Jacob Payne's experience, they were.

Either way, the nickname seemed apt. Lucky had quietly added to his cash over the evening. Jacob didn't always mind losing, but he didn't like seeing one man win that big and that consistently. It took all the fun out of the game.

But he kept his mouth shut.

As the cards landed in front of him, Jacob gently lifted up the corner to see what he had been dealt: four of spades, jack of diamonds, three of clubs, nine of diamonds, seven of hearts.

He kept a close eye on the others as they placed their bets. Lucky seemed confident—maybe that's where his luck came from—but Jacob hadn't been playing with them long enough to be able to read any signs of what kinds of cards they may have in front of them.

It went around again and Jacob drew three new cards, keeping his diamonds but not getting anything new worth a damn. Jacob looked at his dwindling cash and reached a decision. Besides, he didn't want to stick around and listen to more of Abe's griping.

"That's it for me," he said, dropping his cards on the table. "This has been a rich evening, boys."

Abe grinned. "C'mon, stay a bit."

"And give you all more of my money? I don't think

so." Jacob clapped Edwin on the shoulder as he passed. "I'll see you tomorrow."

"You off to the cafe?" Edwin asked with a wink.

Jacob paused. He hadn't actually put the idea to himself, but as soon as Edwin mentioned it he realized that was exactly where he was heading. Having a drink by himself—or maybe in the company of a certain waitress—sounded like the perfect way to end his evening.

At Jacob's silence, Edwin laughed and said, "That's what I thought."

"Good night," the bounty hunter said pointedly on his way out the door.

The San Xavier Cafe was only a short block away from the Golden Saddle Saloon where he had been playing. Tucson was growing, and fast. There was even a rumor that they'd get their own newspaper later that fall. Jacob walked purposefully through the dim streets. The sun had just set. The sounds of drinking and the beginnings of evening entertainment surrounded him.

He was getting tired of this heat. All the Arizona locals had warned him. He'd laughed it off. But they were right and he was wrong. His first summer in Arizona had been a shock. When he was on the trail of an outlaw, focused and determined, he could easily ignore the discomfort. On days like this, however, when he was still trying to find a suitable horse to purchase or waiting for a new tip to come in, the heat was all he could think about. It overwhelmed him and influenced every decision.

Thankfully, with the sun now below the horizon,

the evening was cooler, if only a little. Jacob took off his hat as he stepped through the door of the San Xavier Cafe and fanned his face. He spotted an empty seat at the bar, and was sure to catch the waitress's eye as he sat down.

Bonnie Loft made her way across the room to him with a shy smile. Her dark, almost black, straight hair was pulled back off her face in a low bun, but the tiniest wisps had fallen out to frame her face. Every time she unconsciously reached up to push a strand back behind her ear, he couldn't help but smile at the gesture.

"I haven't seen you all day, Jacob," she said, teasing. "Did you not eat today?"

She ran her small hand across the broad expanse of his back as she crossed behind his seat. Her touch was casual and fleeting, but Jacob knew she wasn't friendly like this with all her customers.

The old Irish bartender appeared in front of Jacob with a neat whiskey. "Usual, eh, Payne?"

"Thanks, Mickey."

"It breaks my poor heart to see you drinking such dodgy rubbish."

"I know." He grinned. "One day we'll go back to Dublin and you can show me the real stuff."

Mickey Sheehan was anywhere from fifty to eighty years old, and spoke with a brogue as thick as molasses. Jacob once heard that the man had been on this continent for going on thirty years, yet still he talked about his home town as if he were going back any day—including how terrible the whiskey was all the way out here on the western side of the continent.

Jacob raised his glass in thanks and took a sip. The warmth that spread through his torso made him feel better about his losses at the saloon. He was improving at poker, though. Maybe tomorrow night he'd try again, if he was still in town.

Bonnie leaned against the bar next to him, watching and waiting for him to be ready to talk. Finally, she said, "Where've you been, Jacob? You've got another bounty to go hunt down?"

"Not yet." He took another small sip and shook his head. "If I had a horse, I could go to Prescott or farther west where there are rumors of cattle rustlers. But in the meantime I just have to wait here for some chance to buy a suitable animal. I'm not used to such limited options."

"There's nothing in town that suits you?"

"I guess I'm just picky. Paint happened across my path on my way out here from Texas and I couldn't have asked for a better horse. Nothing here in Tucson right now even comes close. Maybe I'm just waiting for another perfect horse to wander into my life."

"It is a shame that man shot him."

"Jed Corker?" Jacob stared down into his drink. He was still angry about that outlaw shooting his horse out from under him. He took a beat to calm his temper. "He deserves everything the law can throw at him."

After a moment, Bonnie rested her fingers lightly on his forearm, drawing his attention to her. "Why don't you take my mare, Jacob? She may not be the perfect companion for you forever, but she's a good horse to borrow for a bit. Lord knows I won't need her desperately for a week or so, and she stays cooped up so much of the time. With Franny you can get out of town."

He mulled over the offer. That might be exactly what he needed. For the last month he had been going nonstop. Now that Deputy Lowry didn't have any immediate leads on any of the wanted men in the area, it might be just the time for him to distract himself from the heat for a bit and scout out options elsewhere.

"That's an idea," he said. "Only question left is where I'd go. Down to Mexico?"

She nodded. "Or what about the White Mountains over to the east? I haven't been there myself, but I hear good things. There's rumors of gold being discovered out there. Maybe you can use that good luck of yours and stumble across a couple nuggets."

Jacob chuckled, thinking of his last poker game. "I don't know about luck. I'd settle for just a horse. And being in the mountains does sound nice."

"You didn't have any real mountains back in Virginia, did you?"

"Not near where I lived, but I passed through the Blue Ridge Mountains on my way out here to Arizona. I do miss the forests of back east." He sighed, remembering the rolling hills and dense forests around his family's Virginia farm. He could spend hours out there, just listening to the sounds of farm life, smelling the pine and the rotting leaves underfoot. But, he reminded himself, he had left that farm for a reason. Arizona was his home for the foreseeable future and now was the perfect chance to see some of what it had to offer—other than parched and desolate desert.

"I almost stayed in the White Mountains before coming here, you know," Bonnie said. "It's a beautiful place."

Jacob finished the rest of his whiskey in one long gulp. Now that he had a plan, he was ready to get going. But first, he'd need one last night's sleep in a proper bed.

"You've sold me, Bonnie." He set his glass down and waved Mickey away when the older man came to offer him a second. "If you really can spare her for a couple weeks, I'd be glad to take you up on that offer."

"Well, now I don't know if I want to let her go if that means I won't be seeing you for a couple weeks." She leaned close. "I'm teasing, of course. I'll have her ready and saddled for you here tomorrow morning, if that works for you?"

"I couldn't ask for more." He stood up from his stool and suppressed a desire to hug her, holding her petite body close to him. "That means I have a lot to do before tomorrow, so I'll be saying goodnight."

"Goodnight, Jacob." Bonnie wore a wide smile, but her eyes didn't reflect the same joy as she said goodbye to him. Perhaps she wanted to hug him as well.

By the next morning, Jacob had everything sorted and packed early. He carried it all over to the San Xavier Cafe to meet Bonnie and her mare.

"Is this your girl?" he asked, approaching the gray mottled mare that stood in front of the building.

"Yes, sir. This is Franny." Bonnie fed her horse half of an apple and whispered to her. "She'll be good to you."

"Thanks, Bonnie. I'll bring her back safe and sound in a couple weeks or so."

"You'd better, Jacob Payne. I want you back safe and sound, too."

He kissed her cheek and swung into the saddle. A few days in the mountains, around real, green trees, would refresh him like nothing else could.

Jacob and Franny began their long trek northeast across the desert. Riding toward the sunrise, Jacob felt a fresh new start, a blank slate, and imagined the wide expanse of possibility before him.

Somehow he had missed passing through the White Mountains in eastern Arizona on his way out west earlier that year. The idea that there was still unexplored wilderness everywhere around him was exhilarating. He might be the first man to spot a particular tributary of a river, or witness a wild predator take down its prey. He could be alone in the wilderness, not seeing another human for hours, if not days. He could leave his mark, without competition, without challengers. After all, wasn't this why men left the cities and civilization on the eastern seaboard? Why, in fact, they crossed the Atlantic Ocean to conquer the new continent centuries ago? The untamed wild of the western territories was just sitting there, waiting to be inhabited. And now Jacob would have a chance to claim another piece of it, if only temporarily.

He wasn't sure where exactly he was headed, but he was sure he'd know when he got there. Between Tucson and the mountains were a number of small towns, both mining and railroad, and Jacob aimed to stop in as many of them as he came upon. He'd heard that talking to the men of Globe or introducing himself to the small town sheriff usually yielded information or bounties beyond what most bounty hunters actively sought. Jacob had learned long ago that there were details everywhere if you just paid attention.

Midway through his first day, Jacob rode into a small town of perhaps eight hundred people. The single long main street stretched before him, dry as a bone with dust being kicked up. Men tipped their hats in greeting as he rode past; women smiled at him, welcoming the stranger to town. Jacob thought they must not have had much trouble here if not a single citizen was wary of him.

After making a few inquiries Jacob discovered the town was called Falcon, and he was politely directed to the town livery where he boarded Franny for a few hours. She deserved a nice rest after their long ride, and he could spend the time eating, replenishing his stores, and maybe even resting himself. Jacob was still not used to the idea that he didn't have any outlaws to pursue at this moment. Far more common was a constant alertness, and he had not yet settled in to such a long break.

Another kind soul directed him to the saloon where he could get a drink and a hot meal. As he walked through the door, no fewer than three of the men inside looked up and nodded their hellos. He relaxed the smallest amount as he found a seat and got his food.

As Jacob drained his first beer, an older couple approached his table and introduced themselves. The older man wore a stark white beard, bowler hat, and trim brown suit that reminded Jacob of his father on a Sunday morning. The woman next to him, also with stark white hair under a small hat, hung back half a step, as though used to letting her husband lead the way.

"Good afternoon, sir," the man began, offering his hand for Jacob to shake. "We are so sorry to interrupt your mealtime, but we couldn't help but notice you're a stranger to Falcon."

"I am," Jacob answered cautiously, his relaxation all dried up.

The man gestured to the two empty chairs at the table. "Mind if we sit?"

Jacob nodded.

"My name is John McFadden. I'm the mayor here in Falcon. This is my wife, Constance. What brings you to our humble little town?"

Jacob took a moment to gesture to the bartender for another beer before answering. He tried to hide his smile at the thought that the mayor himself was the personal welcoming committee of this small town.

"I'm just passing through," he said.

"What is it you do, son? Is there anything we can help you with while you're in town? Anyone I can introduce you to?"

"That's very kind of you, Mr. McFadden. But I really am just passing through on my way to the mountains. I'm a bounty hunter by trade—"

Mrs. McFadden interrupted him with a frightened gasp.

"Are you all right, ma'am?"

She seemed unable to speak for a moment.

Her husband cleared his throat. "What was your name, sir?"

"Jacob Payne."

"Mr. Payne," he said, his voice suddenly stern, "we don't want any trouble here. Falcon is a safe, quiet community, and if you're going to be coming into town raising a ruckus, we don't need your kind."

"No, sir." Jacob looked both of his hosts in the eyes. "That's not why I'm here. Quite the opposite. Hunting down an outlaw is serious business, and I treat it as such. I do my duty to capture the renegade and hand him over to the law. On my honor, sir, I have never once had to kill in my line of work. I really am just passing through your town."

She pressed her hand to her bosom, her eyes wide. "Oh, lord, there couldn't possibly be a fugitive here, could there? We've never had such a thing."

He paused before continuing. In his experience, it simply wasn't possible that Falcon would never see trouble, but could he tell her that? Lying was always his last resort, but sometimes it couldn't be helped, especially in order to protect someone. He was always having to weigh his options and judge the lesser of the two evils. Sometimes a little misdirection really was the best option, or sometimes he could sense that they wouldn't hear the truth anyway. Pieces of the truth were often sufficient, and the listener would never need to know what he had held back from them.

"No, ma'am, I'm sure you're perfectly safe here. If you've not had a bank robbery or kidnapping in Falcon, there's no reason to worry."

"Oh, God bless you," she said, exhaling.

He smiled politely and said his goodbyes. Better to get on the road sooner than he had planned than to be roped into another partial truth. He and Franny had plenty more terrain to cover.

The next afternoon, Jacob rode into a town so small he wondered if it even had a name. There appeared to be only two public buildings and half a dozen homes scattered within a three-mile area. He slowed Franny to a casual walk and made his way down the sole street. As he passed one of the two buildings, a rotund man with shaggy gray hair came out into the doorway to greet him.

"You lost, son?" he asked jokingly. "Not many strangers find their way to Cork, Arizona."

Jacob waved in greeting and nudged Franny toward the storefront. "Is that where I am? Cork? I've come from Tucson on my way to the White Mountains and wasn't sure what I'd find in between."

"Yes, sir. You found us. Tie up that gorgeous creature you're riding and let me get you a drink."

"Mighty nice of you," Jacob replied as he dismounted. There was only a single hitching post on this street, but seeing as Jacob was the only one here, that didn't seem to be a problem.

"Come in, come in," the man said. "My name is Marty Colfax."

As they stepped over the threshold, Jacob recognized the shelves and storage of a general store, the tables and chairs of a diner, and the counter and workroom of a post office. Jacob loved these kinds of small towns, where a single man fulfilled three or four different roles for the residents.

A kind-looking woman with a pile of graying brown hair atop her head waited behind the cash register. A young teenage boy came out of the back room wearing an apron and carrying a towel, staring at Jacob as he entered.

"It's a man," the kid said in awe.

Jacob laughed. "Well, Mr. Colfax, you weren't kidding about not many strangers here, were you?"

"No, sir." He pushed ahead of Jacob farther into the room and offered him one of the tables. "I want to say it's been almost a year since anyone new has come through."

"Thirteen months," the kid whispered.

"Ah, yes. Thank you, professor." He remained standing next to Jacob's table as he gestured to the other two. "This is my family. My wife, Hester, and our youngest, Amos. We have one other older boy, Joel, back at home repairing a fence today. And, I'm sorry, I didn't catch your name."

"Jacob Payne," he replied, removing his hat and nodding politely to the woman and child.

"Mind if I sit, Mr. Payne?"

"Not at all. And please call me Jacob."

"Okay then, Jacob." Colfax sat across from him and leaned over the table on his elbows, suddenly staring hard at him. "Now, we are good Christians and we want to offer hospitality to any man that walks through that door. But at the same time, the world is a wicked place and I need to be sure I'm protecting my own."

Jacob nodded slowly. "I understand."

"So I'm going to need you to tell me exactly what you're doing in this backwoods corner of the territory."

"Of course, sir." Jacob clasped his hands on the table, demonstrably away from his weapons. It was such a stark difference from his welcome in Falcon that he couldn't help but respect this man's boldness. "I'm a bounty hunter."

"Oh heavens," Mrs. Colfax interrupted, clutching her neck. "There's an outlaw in Cork?"

"No, ma'am. I'm sorry to scare you," Jacob said, trying to be soothing.

"Then what is it you're doing here, Mr. Payne?" Colfax asked.

"As a matter of fact, I find myself out here *because* there are no bank robbers or murderers for me to chase. I came from Tucson, as I mentioned, and the U.S. Marshal there is doing such a great job that the tips for wanted men are few and far between. So a friend suggested I get out of town and look to see if I can be helpful elsewhere. I'm told the White Mountains boast of some of the most beautiful forests in this part of the world, so I'm on my way there to do

some poking around, check in with the lawmen, and"
—he smiled disarmingly—"maybe even get in some
fishing."

"Guess there's not much opportunity for fishing in
Tucson," Colfax said, finally leaning back in his chair.

"No, sir, there's not."

"So you'll be on your way tomorrow?"

"Yes," Jacob said cautiously. "Unless you'd like me
to go now."

"No, that's not necessary. As I said, we're Christians and we'll feed you and give you a roof. I'd like
you to turn your revolvers over to me while you're
here, if you don't mind. But we have plenty of room in
our barn for you and your horse to stay the night."

Jacob paused briefly before responding. "That
seems fair, sir." He placed his revolvers on the table,
careful to make sure the barrels were not pointed at
his host. The bounty hunter slid the weapons over,
trusting his life and his defenses to a man he had
just met.

In truth, assuming there really was no danger in
Cork, this would be a comfortable, relaxing evening
for him, and if that meant turning over his weapons
for a few hours then he was happy to oblige. In the
few months he had been chasing bad men, Jacob had
learned that sometimes trusting the good ones was
the only way forward.

CHAPTER THREE

Once they made their way to the Colfax homestead, his host showed Jacob to a new barn, clean and warm. With Franny settled in for the night, brushed and watered, Jacob was looking forward to a night of relaxation. He smiled to himself—Bonnie had led him well. So far he'd had no trouble in finding a kind stranger who was willing to help him feel at home.

The two men stood in the doorway of the barn, discussing Jacob's route the next day, farther toward the mountains, and where he could go to best find the fishing he aimed to do. The cool evening breeze wafted across his sweaty brow.

The farmhouse door opened, spilling light across the ground. Mrs. Colfax crossed the dirt yard from the house, carrying a quilt in her arms. "You will probably need this. The nights get cool around here," she called as she drew closer.

"Thank you kindly, ma'am."

"Will you be staying for breakfast?"

Jacob took the armful of fabric from her when she reached the barn. Before he could answer, they were interrupted by the sound of galloping hooves tearing toward the barn from the darkness.

"Mr. Parr!" Colfax said as the rider drew closer. "What on earth are you doing here at this time of night?"

The horse slowed as it approached the barn, and Jacob noticed the man's saddlebags and supplies seemed to be minimal. Either this man was counting on the kindness of strangers, or he expected a quick journey.

"I've been sent to get word to the U.S. Marshal's office," the man said, panting a little as he climbed down off his horse.

Jacob jumped into action, helping the man bring the exhausted horse inside, remove the saddle, make sure it had water, and take care of the animal as best he could. He heard Marty Colfax gently suggest to his wife that she return to the house. While Jacob worked, he and Marty asked the man more questions.

"What happened to your telegraph office?" Marty asked. "I would have thought that'd be easier than tearing across the country."

Parr shook his head. "Blasted Pickens cut the wire. We didn't even realize until a couple hours went by with no response. He gave himself a head start."

"Who did?" Jacob asked.

"I think his name is Pickens. Or maybe Picketts? I'm not certain. He weren't in Elk Springs too long."

"That name sound familiar to you?" Colfax asked Jacob.

He searched his memory but shook his head. If this man was wanted for a crime, it wasn't anywhere in the Arizona Territory that he knew of. Or under either one of those names, at least.

"What did he do, Parr?" Colfax asked quietly, checking behind him to be sure his wife had gone.

"One of the Kimball ladies has been kidnapped."

"I'll go," Jacob said resolutely. "I'll find her."

"And who the hell are you?" Parr said, his voice full of accusation. He seemed to have finally recognized that he had no idea who he had divulged all this information to.

"This man is a bounty hunter," Colfax clarified for his friend. "Let him help."

Parr nodded reluctantly. "All right. If you say so. But trusting strangers is what got us into this mess."

Colfax led them into the house where Mrs. Colfax had already returned and started a pot of coffee. The kitchen table was clear, save for the older boy, Joel, tucked into the corner reading his Bible. He seemed all arms and legs to Jacob, right at that age where his body was still growing but before the mass of muscle had filled in.

"You're fine, son," Marty said when the boy moved to vacate his chair. "You're old enough to hear this."

"Mr. Parr," Jacob began as the men sat. "I need you to tell me everything you know."

Mrs. Colfax placed mugs of coffee in front of each of them and Parr pulled out a flask to add a little something extra to his. He took a sip, shook his head as though clearing the cobwebs from his brain, took a deep breath, and began.

"This man—Pickens, Picketts, whatever—he showed up in Elk Springs four or five days ago. Not many. Claimed he's from St. Louis and was looking for the rumored Herron Gold Mine. Now, of course, there's no telling if any of that is true. As far as I can tell, he asked around, got friendly with a number of the families, and had everyone just eating out of his hand, easy as you please."

"How many people are in Elk Springs?" Jacob asked.

Mr. Parr thought a moment. "I'd say near five hundred."

"And the men have already formed a posse?"

He grimaced. "When I left, a couple of them were trying. But there aren't many men willing to stick their necks out for the Kimballs."

"Why?" Jacob asked, bewildered.

"Excuse me," Joel said, quietly but firmly interrupting. "Did you say the Kimballs?"

"Yes," Mr. Parr said to the boy. He turned his attention back to Jacob. "The Kimball family is Mormon. That alone makes them a bit queer, but they also live about three miles or so outside of town and don't associate with us regular." He shrugged.

"So, because they worship a bit differently, there are people in Elk Springs willing to let them be kidnapped?" Jacob tried to keep the accusation out of his voice. The poker game of the night before, with that idiot Abe, flashed in his mind.

"Well, now," Parr said defensively, "if it were just a matter of one of them breaking a leg or needing help with the cattle, the people of Elk Springs would jump to help out their neighbor. But rescuing from a devil?"

Mrs. Colfax approached the table with two mugs of steaming hot coffee in each hand, set them gently on the surface, and handed one to each man in turn. Jacob thanked her as he received his, taking a deep whiff of the rich aroma.

"You can't blame them for wanting to stay safe," Colfax said, sipping from his own mug.

"Right." Jacob recognized it was easier to acquiesce even if he didn't agree. "Are there any leads? Any idea where he's gone with the victim?"

"Mr. Kimball says he followed the horse tracks as far as the river, and then lost them. But they were headed north. The same direction as the rumored gold mine."

"When you say 'rumored'—"

"It don't exist," Parr said emphatically. "Half of Elk Springs settled there because they were looking for that mine, and if none of us could find it in the last couple years then it ain't there."

"But does *Pickens* know that?"

"Could be. Could be he wants to look himself. Could be he was just using that as an excuse to talk to the women."

"What happened that made him snap and take the girl?"

Parr shook his head. "I don't know. I didn't have a chance to do no investigating before I came tearing down the mountain. All I know is a young girl like Flora . . ." He trailed off, glancing warily at Joel.

Jacob knew what he was thinking without it

having to be said out loud—what they all were thinking. The risk of a girl like that, of any female, in the company of and under the control of a man like that . . . well, in all likelihood, if she lived through the event she'd never be the same.

"You aiming to go after her, Payne?" Colfax asked.

Jacob nodded.

Colfax turned to Parr. "In the morning you can go on to Desierto, where I'm sure they have a telegraph office, but that may be too late for Flora."

"I want to go," Joel said from his corner. Jacob had almost forgotten he was sitting there. "I'm going too."

"Honey, I don't think—" his mother began.

"I have to go, Mother. I have to. It's Flora." The pleading and heartbreak in his voice was unmistakable. "Mr. Payne will find Elk Springs quicker with me to guide him. We can't lose any time."

"Joel," Colfax said, "I don't want you getting yourself tangled up with any outlaw."

"I'm a grown man, Father. And you've said yourself we're Christians who try to do good by our neighbors. If the men in Elk Springs, who all have wives and children to support, won't go, then someone like me should. Flora needs help."

The boy's parents exchanged a glance. Jacob witnessed them have what amounted to a fully silent conversation, just communicating with a twist of an eyebrow and shrug of a shoulder.

"You're right, son," Marty finally said. "If it don't bother Mr. Payne none, your mother and I will consent to you going."

Jacob was torn. He liked to work alone while he

was on the trail, not have to be responsible for anyone else. But this boy—this young man—was clearly desperate to accompany him. He might try following no matter what he's told.

"I can't vouch for your safety, Joel. It will be rough and dangerous. Not only is there a chance we might fail, but there's always a chance we might die. Are your parents prepared for that? Are you?"

Joel closed his Bible and rested it on the table. "I am, sir."

"Well, then." Jacob nodded. "Let's make whatever preparations we can. We'll leave at dawn."

The next day Jacob found himself on Franny, following Joel through the sparse pine trees on the slight incline up the mountains, as the sun came peeking over the horizon. They had left the Colfax homestead still in the predawn dark and made steady progress through the foothills. In spite of the danger of the mission ahead, Jacob was elated to be back among the evergreens.

"It's not much farther," Joel called over his shoulder. "We should get there well before supper, I think."

"How often do you travel to Elk Springs?" Jacob asked.

"Pretty often."

"You know the Kimballs?"

Joel didn't respond initially, but eventually he slowed his horse to walk alongside Jacob's. "Maybe Father didn't mention this last night, but my family used to live in Elk Springs. Amos and me were both born there. We moved down to Cork when I was about fourteen, but I've known Flora Kimball since they got to Elk Springs. Most of our lives, I'd say."

Jacob waited for the boy to say more. He had learned there were some people who just needed space and to be allowed to take their time, rather than pressing them with specific questions.

But he never did. Instead, Joel gave him a pinched smile, flicked his reins, and rode on ahead. Whatever place the girl held in his heart, Joel was keeping her close.

The incline was getting steeper now, the trail more narrow. At times Jacob lost sight of it completely, but Joel seemed to know where they were going. They rode one behind the other, instead of side by side, and stayed quiet, each listening to the forest around them.

After some time, above him Jacob heard a creaking sound. He tried to turn to see what it was, but the mare was skittish at the sound.

"Shhh, it's okay," he said. But in that moment, when Jacob turned his attention to the horse, he missed the five-foot-long branch as it came crashing to the ground just next to them.

Franny bolted.

The second the enormous branch crashed to the ground, Bonnie's mare, Franny, tore through the unfamiliar woods at a gallop. Jacob clenched his teeth, but he willed himself to relax into the mare's stride. It had been a long time since a horse of his had spooked. He didn't want to hurt her or scare her more, but he needed to calm the horse and get her back under his control.

Why hadn't Bonnie warned him that her horse was high-strung? He might not have taken her on this journey if he had known. This was the first time he could remember being angry with the woman, but this was the worst thing that could happen. Jacob couldn't be dealing with this, looking after a young man and worrying about the mare when he was hunting down a kidnapper.

Franny wove between the tree trunks, seemingly without destination or thought to how far she was taking her rider away from the trail. Jacob took deep, slow breaths, talking calmly to Franny and letting her lead until he could calm her down. He reached forward to stroke her mane, placing his broad hand on the tense muscles of her neck.

After some time her frantic gallop slowed to a trot, and finally Jacob was able to guide her to stopping altogether. He dismounted and spoke soothingly to Franny, his low voice helping to slow her heart rate. The poor girl was petrified, and even through his frustration he couldn't blame her. He wondered when was the last time she had even seen a tree, let alone had one almost fall on her. It took a few minutes for her to stop trembling, but she seemed to trust Jacob enough to allow herself to be led back through the trees, back toward where they came from.

Jacob was far off the trail now. During Franny's frantic run, he hadn't been paying attention to where they went or what landmarks they passed. He had a pretty good idea, though, and Jacob stepped over fallen branches and through undergrowth toward where he thought Joel might be.

"Hello!" he cried. If he could just get within the boy's hearing, he could easily find the trail. "Joel?"

There was no response, but Jacob kept moving forward, eyes open for any indication of a path to Elk Springs. There would have to be more than one path around here, right? The town wasn't a fortress or stronghold. Somewhere nearby there must be some indication of humans making their mark on the wilderness.

But after twenty minutes of walking through trees, Jacob still didn't see anything familiar. The broken branches and other signs that he might use to track an outlaw weren't enough for him to trust it as a path back to civilization. He thought for sure he would have come upon the trail or the boy by now.

After another five minutes of walking without finding another clue, Jacob finally admitted to himself that he was lost. Deep in the trees as he was, it was difficult to even see where the sun was. But at least he knew that uphill would be east. Or, it *should* be east. Why didn't he think to get more specific directions from Joel? Why hadn't he considered the fact that they might get separated?

"Joel Colfax!" he yelled again.

He wasn't afraid of making noise. After all, the more noise he made the less likely he was to be surprised by a bear or whatever other predators might be in these mountains. Were there bears in Arizona? Mountain lions? There must be. Just another question he should have asked before setting off to some unknown terrain.

Franny kept close to him, nudging at his collar periodically. Maybe she sensed animals outside Jacob's range of sight. Or maybe she just was afraid of another branch falling. Either way, Jacob kept a comforting hand on her as they tried to find the trail again.

He kept moving in the direction he thought was south, along the length of the mountainside rather than farther up or downhill. He was certain that eventually he'd find something that would help him get his bearings.

Jacob took a deep breath, filled his lungs, and yelled as loud as he could. "Hello!"

"Hello?" a tiny voice answered him.

Jacob couldn't be certain where it was coming from so he yelled again. "Joel?"

"Mr. Payne?"

That second response floated down to him from uphill. Jacob's stomach sank as he realized he had been going the wrong direction. If he had not heard the voice at that moment, he may have wandered around the mountainside for hours more.

"Keep yelling, Joel," he called, relieved.

"Hello!"

Joel periodically shouted to Jacob, often enough that the bounty hunter was able to put himself in the right direction, heading uphill toward where the boy waited for him. He continued to lead the horse on foot until they finally reached the trail.

When Joel came within his sight, Jacob noted the tree branch on the path. "Did you just wait here for me?"

The boy nodded. "Is that all right? I thought I probably shouldn't move off the trail in case you came back."

"That's perfect. Let's hope nothing else spooks this girl."

"Yeah." Joel furrowed his brow. "Is she going to be okay?"

"I dunno. She's not my horse, so I'm not sure. I'd hate for her to become a problem on the trail."

"You can't— I mean, um," Joel stammered. "What

I'm trying to say, sir, respectfully, is that I'm worried. I can't let anything stop us from rescuing Flora."

"I know, Joel. I'll figure it out." He swung back into the saddle and nudged Franny forward. "Are we close?"

"Yep. Should be. I think only another ten minutes or so."

It was even less time than that before Jacob smelled the distinctive scent of a cooking fire. A couple of them, he thought. That thick smokiness mixed with the delicious aroma of roasting meat guided them. All of a sudden, Jacob realized he was starving. Whatever it was, he couldn't wait to eat it.

The trail leveled out as the trees thinned. The mountain continued to climb ahead of them, with the town of Elk Springs nestled into a small hollow on the mountainside. It wasn't yet sunset, but many of the buildings they passed shone from within with lantern light. The warm, pleasant glow of suppertime welcomed the two travelers.

"We can stop at the tavern," Joel said. "Follow me."

Before they got much farther, though, they were stopped in the middle of the road by a group of men. A tall man led the group. He wore his blond mustache long and unkempt, connected to his sideburns. The man glowered at the newcomers from under his hat as he stalked toward them. The rest of his group followed closely and casually but visibly held their guns. Shotguns, revolvers, and pistols rested in hands ready to pull the trigger if needed.

Jacob reined in Franny, slowing to a stop at Joel's side.

"Joel Colfax?" the mustached man in front asked. "Is that you? What are you doing here? What are you doing with this stranger?" He glared at Jacob, who silently met his gaze.

"Mr. Parr showed up at our place, Sheriff Dale," Joel said. "He told us what happened to Flora. Me and Mr. Payne have come to help."

"Mr. Payne, huh?" the man asked, still glaring at Jacob.

"That's right," he said. "Jacob Payne."

The sheriff walked closer to them, and Jacob silently willed Franny to stay calm and not get spooked again. "What makes you think we want your help?"

"I'm a bounty hunter and have some experience tracking down wanted men. I'm happy to help if I can."

The man looked skeptical, but was interrupted when one of the others in the group spoke up. "Let's get these fellas fed, anyway, Chester. They musta had a long ride from Cork. We'll fill Mr. Payne in on the situation and then he can decide if he still wants to help."

Jacob tried to get a sign from Joel about what he thought, but the boy was trembling with fury. Clearly something in this short exchange had upset him greatly.

"That's mighty kind of you," Jacob answered for both of them.

Just a few minutes later, Jacob found his horse

safely boarded in the Elk Springs livery and Joel and himself seated at a long table in the Elk Springs Tavern, surrounded by the armed welcoming committee.

"Dig in, boys," said the sheriff. "I know you been on the road all day."

Jacob gladly took his first bite. The smoked elk and potatoes were warm and satisfying after following its smell on their approach up the mountain. He took a few more filling bites before he broke the silence with his questions.

"Could you men fill us in on what has been done to rescue Miss Kimball? What are we dealing with and what do we already know?"

"*Miss* Kimball." The man on the end snorted with suppressed laughter.

"Is that funny?" Jacob asked.

"It's Mrs. Kimball," the man called Chester clarified. He was seated directly across the table from Jacob and Joel. He had been called sheriff earlier, and seemed to be the leader of this party.

"I'm sorry." Jacob looked from one man's face to the other. "I just assumed she was a daughter, since she's younger than Joel."

"She *is* the daughter," Joel said emphatically.

"I don't know about that," Chester said condescendingly. "Those Mormons are known for taking more than one wife. Why else would this Kimball fellow live way out in the wild like he does, if he were living like normal folk?"

"What?" Joel spluttered angrily. "What are you

talking about? I've known the Kimballs since I was five years old. They are exactly like you and me."

"That may be, son, but that don't mean you know the whole truth."

"He doesn't know what he's talking about," Joel said to Jacob. "Flora and her sister, Edith, their mother died when they were young. The new Mrs. Kimball is their stepmother. Not their sister-wife or whatever they're called."

"Do you know why they live so far away from the rest of the town?" Jacob asked. He had to admit that did seem suspicious. Living so far away from help and supplies was a big risk. There must be a reason for it.

"Wouldn't you if you had to live with such closed-minded, un-Christian pigs like these?" Joel gestured to the man sitting opposite, clearly not caring that the man could hear every word and criticism thrown his way.

"Boy," the sheriff said, "you watch your tone. Maybe she is Kimball's daughter. But those folks are real queer, and we don't know he didn't take her as a wife, too."

Many of the other men at the table shifted in their seats, shooting looks to each other and shaking their heads. Jacob felt the room shift, away from the sheriff, distancing him and his ideas from the rest of the group. Jacob suspected that they were willing to follow him if it meant not having to go after an outlaw, but they still couldn't hold with calling their neighbor names.

"Now, Chester." The same man who had soothed him earlier spoke up. "That's a mighty strong accusation. Let's not speak ill of our neighbor without any kind of proof."

"I don't need proof. I can tell."

"You don't know anything," Joel said coldly. "Flora Kimball is kind and pure, and at this very moment she is in the clutches of a madman. We have to go after her."

"We'll not be going in the dark, though," Jacob reminded him. "So let's get back to the discussion of what has been done and what you boys already know."

There was a perceptible pause while all in attendance waited to see if Chester wanted to speak. When he continued to shovel food into his mouth angrily, the man to his right spoke up.

"We haven't actually gone after her at all," the man said quietly, looking down at his plate. He quickly took a bite, filling his mouth with food so he couldn't be expected to say more.

"What?" Joel said, aghast. "I thought— I mean, Mr. Parr came tearing into Cork yesterday. He made it sound like you were treating this as an emergency. What have you been doing all day?"

"We are treating it as an emergency. That is, we did. To the extent that we contacted the U.S. Marshal."

Jacob almost wondered if he had misheard the man. He looked from one man to another, trying to ascertain exactly what he was dealing with, who was calling the shots, and how much help he could expect from them going forward. To their credit, all of the men aside from the sheriff seemed at least a little embarrassed by their lack of action. Staying safe and comfortable was one thing; acting cowardly was quite another.

"Start at the beginning," he said firmly.

When no one spoke up, Joel prompted, "Mr. Parr told us that this man showed up a few days ago asking about the Herron Gold Mine?"

Each of the six men traded glances. Jacob thought he felt one of them kicking another under the table, but still no one spoke up. Three of the men took large bites of their meal and averted their eyes. Without specific details of the girl's kidnapping and what information the outlaw might be working with, Jacob despaired of finding her easily. He looked from one Elk Springs man to another, waiting for one of them to step up and volunteer details.

Sheriff Dale finally acquiesced, but only to volunteer another man. "Arnie, you're the first one who talked to him. You tell Mr. Payne about what he said to you."

The cluster of men looked at the thin, gangly young man at the corner of the table. Jacob followed their gaze expectantly, trying to hide his impatience. Arnie put his fork down and pushed his plate away from him. He took a deep breath.

"Yeah, so—" He cleared his throat. "This Pickens character showed up here a few days ago. We get some strangers in town from time to time, since Elk Springs is the biggest place on the mountain. He came into my store, asking for rope, a pick axe, and some other things. I think I musta been the first person to talk to him. While he picked out the supplies he needed, he made small talk about the rumored mine, like most strangers do. I didn't think anything more about it.

"I think I told him everything I know. I wasn't in Elk Springs at the peak of the mine-searching, but I know some of the history. I, um . . ." He looked at the sheriff, who nodded his encouragement. "I gave Pickens the names of Kimball and Colfax, who, to my understanding, had searched for the mine the most."

Joel gasped and started coughing, as though choking on a bite. Jacob pounded on his back a couple times before the boy could gasp out, "You gave him my father's name?"

Arnie nodded apologetically. "You have to understand, I didn't mean no harm by it. Your father ain't even 'round here no more. I thought this man was just like every other would-be miner come through here searching after a dream. I couldn't help him, but I could send him on his way."

Joel's anger could be felt like a wave coming off of him, so Jacob interrupted with another question, lest the boy start yelling.

"That was the last time you saw him?"

"No, not exactly. Over the next two or three days we saw him go in the saloon, the livery, make small talk with the women who came into town to do their own shopping. He sent a telegram to someone in Santa Fe, then hovered in the office for another couple hours, eavesdropping and asking questions.

"He must've gotten the name Kimball from a couple people, not just me, because yesterday morning he went out to their place. It's a good three miles or so out of town. He definitely went there looking for something particular."

"And you've talked to Mr. Kimball about this?" Jacob asked.

"I'm getting to that," Arnie said, holding his hands up to ward off any further questions.

The bearded man sitting next to him jumped in. "Yesterday, just before lunchtime, Kimball himself comes tearing into town yelling for help and riding straight to the sheriff's office." He looked pointedly at Dale. "He was hollering about Flora getting kidnapped."

"And then you all formed a posse and went after her, right?" Joel looked anxiously from one face to another. "You went after her right away, right? Tell me you started immediately. She's only seventeen."

Arnie shook his head, looking embarrassed. "You gotta understand, none of us know Flora. Kimball only ever comes into town by himself and leaves the rest of his family out on the property. Boyd here has glimpsed a few of Kimball's women from afar, when they're out in the garden and he rides out to check trap lines."

Joel's fury was growing. "What does that have to do with anything? Even if you didn't know her, she still needs your help. Why would you not give your neighbor whatever aid you can? Isn't that the Christian thing to do?"

There was an awkward silence as each of the men avoided meeting the eyes of either Joel or Jacob. A heavy silence had fallen over the group. Jacob noticed one of the men fidgeting with the buttons on his vest, another flicking nonexistent dust from his hat.

They were hiding something. Jacob needed to know what it was.

He began quietly, trying to keep the accusation out of his voice. "I suspect there's something different about the Kimballs, some reason for hesitation from a community that would otherwise do everything they can."

"There's nothing different about them," Joel protested. "They're the most honorable family I know."

The silence persisted, until the sheriff happened to peek up and catch Jacob's eye. He fixed on the man an expression of such determination that he finally spoke.

"Well." He cleared his throat and sat up straighter. "You see. Reverend Fowler had the idea that maybe the girl being kidnapped was a judgment on Kimball for taking multiple wives."

"What?" Joel shouted.

Jacob put his hand on the boy's shoulder to keep him from leaping completely out of his seat and knocking over the table.

"We didn't want to go against the Lord's will," Sheriff Dale muttered by way of explanation.

Jacob glanced at the young man next to him. It looked as though Joel had been shocked into silence. He sat gaping, open-mouthed, at the group of men sitting around him. He had been so well trained to respect his elders, he didn't appear to even know how to react when faced with such a situation.

For Jacob's part, he had found that keeping his temper usually led to more cooperation from whoever he was angry with. But in this situation it was a struggle.

"I see," he said. "And this Reverend Fowler knows the Kimballs well? And you all trust him to show you the will of God in this?"

"He is a man of God," Sheriff Dale said indignantly. "Who are we to doubt him?"

"The reverend does know the Kimballs," Boyd clarified. "He rides out to their place maybe once a week to try to preach and show them the true way of the Lord."

"He goes out of his way to make that family feel shamed?" Jacob clarified.

"If he really knew them," Joel muttered, "he'd know that Flora is Mr. Kimball's daughter."

"Well, maybe he's done taken a daughter as a wife," the sheriff retorted. "Those folks're known to disregard all of the laws of both God and man."

"He wouldn't," Joel said. "He would never. They would never. Mr. Kimball is a good man."

"How long has it been since you lived here, boy?" the sheriff asked. "A lot can happen given enough time."

"I know Mr. Kimball better than any of you. He helped my family and treated me like a son when I was little. And I was just there visiting less than a year ago."

"And during that year," Dale persisted, "maybe he took his daughter as his wife. Or maybe he done something else. We don't know. The Lord works in mysterious ways, and you'll notice it was none of our daughters been kidnapped."

"I think we're losing the thread," Jacob said, taking control of the situation again. "Setting aside the reverend for a moment, let's go back to when Mr. Kimball came riding into town."

The sheriff sat up straight, confident in his part of the story. "He came straight to jail, told me what happened, and rode home again. Claimed he needed to make sure the rest of his family stayed safe in case Pickens came back."

"And that's when you consulted with Reverend Fowler?"

He nodded. "He advised that we not risk any other lives on behalf of the sinners, so we don't draw God's judgment on ourselves."

Jacob barely resisted rolling his eyes.

"We didn't ignore it completely, though," the short, stocky man on the end said. "We sent for help."

"True," the sheriff said with a nod. "We sent a wire to Tucson. She had been gone for a couple hours already, but we didn't want there to be any blowback from the law. We did our part. It wasn't until a couple hours later when Mrs. Merrill insisted she was still expecting a wire from her sister in Kansas City that we suspected the communications weren't going through. Sure enough, Boyd here climbed atop the telegraph office to investigate and found the wires cut."

"It took you all day to notice your wire had been cut?" Joel asked.

Jacob marveled that the once quiet and respectful boy was now taking these men to task.

Dale held his hands up defensively. "Well, now, hold on, Joel. Elk Springs is not a busy place. Sometimes we go days without using that machine. There's no way to know exactly when he made the cut, but we suspect Pickens probably did it just before he took the girl.

"So, then, Parr left to get word to the lawmen and . . ." He trailed off. "And then the next day you two showed up."

Joel groaned and leaned forward, resting his forehead on the unfinished wooden table.

Jacob nodded, his mind racing at all the things he had to do to clean up this mess the men of Elk Springs had created—or at least let fester by doing less than nothing. He didn't say anything, but sat up and continued to eat, putting forkfuls in his mouth and thinking while every man at the table watched him for a reaction.

The first thing they needed to do was figure out where Pickens might have taken the girl. And why. Why Flora? He assumed she was an attractive young woman, given Joel's seeming devotion, which could be reason enough for a man like Pickens to kidnap her. He didn't want to think about what that meant for Flora's prospects, including her chances of survival. He would deal with that later. Once she had been found.

The next thing they had to do—and Jacob groaned inwardly at this realization—was find a different horse for him to borrow. Franny would have been perfectly fine for a few days away from town, but Jacob was no longer on that track. The poor, sensitive mare was in no state to chase down an outlaw. Jacob needed a reliable animal, familiar with the area and less easily agitated.

"Well, gentlemen," Jacob said as he pushed back his chair and stood. "Mr. Colfax and I are going to find Flora Kimball. You can stay put in Elk Springs, going about your regular business, telling yourself the Kimballs don't deserve your help. Or you can set aside your prejudice and join us in rescuing a helpless girl before something worse happens to her."

Jacob wasn't one for making speeches, and he felt self-conscious the entire time those six sets of eyes were on him. But it needed to be said. These men were being selfish and hard-hearted, and that poor girl must be scared out of her mind.

He could help her. They could save her. But they needed to get moving.

Joel stood up next to him, also searching the faces of the other men for some sign that Jacob's words had gotten through to them.

Most of them shook their heads or continued eating with their eyes down, not looking at Jacob. But Jacob caught two of the men whispering to each other at the far end of the table. He couldn't hear what was being said, but neither man seemed defiant.

"We'll be off now," Jacob said. "If you change your mind, we'll still take your help at any time. Come on, Joel."

"Wait. We're coming with you."

Jacob was already at the doorway of the Elk Springs Tavern when he heard himself being called back. He turned to see the two men who had been whispering moments before stand up, throw cash down on the table, and move to join him.

"Wait for us," the shorter one said.

The other men watched them go. Jacob felt another stab of disappointment in their behavior. A man should be generous and brave. Even if he thought a neighbor was strange, that shouldn't stop him from keeping the neighbor's daughter safe. But, Jacob reflected, it takes all kinds to make this world, and if some men weren't unscrupulous then he would eventually find himself out of work.

Jacob nodded and gestured for the two men to join them outside.

Standing on the boardwalk lining the dusty street, the shorter one of the two men shook Jacob's hand. "Hey. Name's Zeke. Ezekiel Boyer. And this is my brother-in-law, Boyd Brannigan."

"What can I do for you, gentlemen? I think I made it clear that this young man and I have things to do."

"Right. You did. And we'd like to help. We know Kimball a fair amount and we don't believe what the reverend is claiming."

"And, besides," Boyd put in, "even if it was true, that girl still needs help."

"So we want to go with you. Just tell us what to do."

Jacob looked at Joel, who shrugged. The bounty hunter preferred to work alone, but it looked now as though he'd somehow formed himself a posse. He'd been sincere when entreating the other men to help. If Joel and Zeke and Boyd did actually follow his directions, maybe he could get use out of them.

"All right. Thank you for doing what's right. But from here on, you do exactly as I say at all times. No questions, no protests. Got it?"

They both nodded.

"Let's start with any information you have that might not have been mentioned in there." Jacob gestured with a tip of his chin. "Any thoughts about where to start?"

Boyd spoke up. "I keep coming back to what Sheriff said. He pointed out that it was Kimball's daughter who was kidnapped, not anyone else's. Why is that? Why is Flora special?"

"That's right, isn't there another girl?" Zeke asked. "I think I heard there are two older daughters. Why this one and not the other?"

"Edith," Joel said, nodding. "She's fifteen, I think."

"Could have just been a matter of access. Maybe Flora was just isolated at the exact right time for him to strike," Jacob said. "But you're right. I think that's a good place to start. We're going to have to find the start of the trail to go after him, and maybe we can get some answers once we're there.

"Joel, you know Mr. Kimball the best. Do you think he'd put us up for the night?"

The boy nodded eagerly. "He would. But we

should get moving. It's almost an hour's ride out to their place."

Jacob let Joel lead the string of riders out the several miles to Kimball's farm. This stretch of forest looked much the same as the trail and forest they passed through to get to Elk Springs. Jacob spent a very tense hour waiting for some small sound to spook Franny and send them galloping away in the wrong direction. The men stayed quiet on the ride out to the farm, each lost in his own thoughts about the following day, which would be spent chasing the trail of an outlaw.

"Hello, the house!" Joel called as they approached. "Mr. Kimball?"

The front door of the home swung open, revealing a silhouetted figure in the doorway. The figure appeared to be a hulking man, bareheaded but holding a shotgun ready. It occurred to Jacob that if this was Mr. Kimball, Pickens must have been out of his mind to risk kidnapping his daughter.

"Who's there?"

"It's me, Mr. Kimball," Joel said, raising his hand to wave. "Joel Colfax. We heard about Flora and I brought some help."

"Joel? Boy, I haven't seen you in months. Come in."

As soon as he stepped back out of the doorway the light spilled across his face; Jacob saw the gentle, careworn face of a worried father instead of the menacing patriarch that had been there a moment before.

The four horses were ground-tied in front of the

porch, and the men stepped cautiously into the house. Disturbing a family's grief was a difficult thing. They were there to help, to offer hope, but at the same time they didn't want to dismiss or diminish the pain that the members of the family might be feeling.

"Ah, Mr. Brannigan. Mr. Boyer," Kimball said as they entered. "It is good of you to assist. I know what Reverend Fowler has been saying about my family, and I know it must be difficult for you to go against the community.

"But who's your friend?" he asked, looking piercingly at Jacob. "I don't believe you're from Elk Springs."

"No, sir." Jacob doffed his hat and offered his hand. "Name's Jacob Payne."

"He's a bounty hunter," Joel said. "He was passing through Cork when we heard about Flora and agreed to come with me."

Jacob smiled at this slight revision of history, but he let the boy have his claim. Truth be told, Joel likely would have come with or without Jacob anyway.

"Who is it, Father?" a small, sweet voice called from the doorway.

"Come in here, Mary. Come say hello to Joel Colfax and his friends. They're here about Flora."

A petite woman, not much older than Jacob, entered the room from the hallway. She gripped her skirt, as though to anchor herself in the space.

"Gentlemen, may I introduce my wife?"

"Oh," she gasped, clasping her hands to her chest. "Are you really here for Flora? Can you find her?"

Jacob nodded. "I think we can, ma'am. But we

have some questions, and we were hoping it wouldn't be too much of an imposition . . ."

"We'll help any way we can. I'm not sure we know anything, though." Mary sat primly on the edge of the rigid chair.

"You might be surprised about what kind of details will help." Jacob pulled his chair closer to where the woman sat. "Take me back to when Pickens showed up here."

She looked at her husband, and he gestured for her to go ahead.

"Mr. Payne, you mustn't think me weak or foolish. We don't know the face of every man that lives in Elk Springs. It didn't occur to me until he had already been here a while that Mr. Pickens might be a stranger."

"I don't think you're foolish at all. I imagine he made himself mighty handy and ingratiating when he got here, didn't he?"

She nodded. "He did."

"How did it happen?"

"Well . . ." She fidgeted, smoothing the fabric of her skirt more than needed. "My husband was out past the pasture, breaking down a tree stump. Mr. Pickens had promised to help, but had found many reasons to stay around the house. He'd busy himself with all sorts of tasks and never make it out to where he was actually needed. It wasn't until after I sent Flora out to the chicken coop that I realized Mr. Pickens was gone, too."

Her husband moved to behind her chair and rested his hand on her shoulder. She reached up to lightly touch his fingers, acknowledging the comfort. It did Jacob's heart good to see such tenderness between the two. For another couple, there might be anger or blame, but the Kimballs seemed united in their pain.

"And when you sent Flora out to get the eggs, that's when he took her?"

Mrs. Kimball nodded. She looked ready to cry, to Jacob's eyes, but held herself together. "I didn't hear any of it," she said in a whisper. "My husband was even farther away. Thank goodness Edith was out near the well at the time and heard the screaming."

Jacob looked around the room, but noticed the other teenage girl was nowhere in sight. "And is Edith okay? Was she attacked as well?"

"No, no. The poor dear is just in shock. She's been in bed since it happened. We've told her it's not her fault and she couldn't have stopped him. But she feels responsible."

"That's ridiculous," Joel said indignantly. "I'll talk to her."

"Not now," Jacob said under his breath. "Let's wait till we find her sister."

"Edith even followed them for a spell, but couldn't keep up. Thank the Lord above. I can't bear to think about losing them both."

"So, then, Edith knows where they went?" Jacob looked hopefully at Mr. Kimball.

He nodded. "She says Pickens was dragging her down the trail that continues up the mountain behind my place." He added to Joel, "The one you all used to explore back in the day."

The young man's eyes grew wide and he stood up excitedly. "Our trail? I know where that is! I can find her."

Jacob, too, felt the first glimmer of hope in the whole affair. "We'll find her, Mr. Kimball. I promise."

He believed his own words to be true . . . but he hoped they would also find her alive and unharmed.

Jacob woke before dawn, rolling over in the hay and staring up at the roof of the barn. The deep navy-blue night sky was just beginning to grow lighter through the gaps in the walls. The Kimballs' rooster out in the chicken coop was beginning his morning ritual. The four men would need to be on the trail as soon as possible. Since they had already missed the prime window immediately after the kidnapping, it'd be best to do this as prudently and carefully as possible.

As he rolled over and got to his knees, Jacob thought he heard the gentle thuds of horse hooves approaching the barn. Immediately he wrapped his fingers around the handle of his revolver. Who would be riding up to this out-of-the-way farm so early in the morning unless they meant to catch the family unawares?

"What—?" Joel said as he woke.

"Shh," Jacob warned, gesturing for the boy to stay down as he crept to the wall of the barn. There, right about the height of his eyes, was a small gap in the boards. The bounty hunter held his gun ready and watched for the approaching stranger.

Within seconds, both Boyd and Zeke were armed and at his side, waiting for whatever Jacob instructed them to do.

The horse and rider got closer. Through the narrow crack, Jacob watched a stranger dressed all in black approach the house, slowing as he got closer, eyes darting in every direction looking for something. He didn't announce himself. He didn't make a sound as he dismounted. He drew his gun and crept toward the house slowly.

Jacob didn't like it one bit.

Just as he was about to confront the stranger, next to him Zeke said, bewilderedly, "That's Reverend Fowler."

"You're sure?"

He nodded.

"Go greet him," Jacob instructed. "He needs to know he's not alone."

He waited in the dark barn, watching carefully as Zeke rounded the corner, exited through the wide door, and called to the new arrival.

"Reverend Fowler! What are you doing here?"

The man in black started, surprised to be seen at all, let alone spoken to. "What? I—"

"You wouldn't be here looking to join our posse, would you?"

"Of course not." The reverend seemed offended at the suggestion.

Jacob stepped out through to doorway, revolver in

hand, eyes boring into the newcomer. "Then what is it we can help you with?"

"I . . . well, I . . ." he spluttered. The reverend closed his mouth, stood up straighter, and adjusted his coat. "I've come to offer my condolences to Mr. Kimball for his loss and extend to him the path to the kingdom of heaven before it's too late."

Jacob held back a bark of laughter. "Fine," he said. "Let's go see what Mr. Kimball has to say about that."

"No, I—"

"Oh, we're going with you, Mister—Fowler, is it? We need to speak to the man before we leave to rescue his daughter. I'm sure he won't mind having us both there."

Jacob grabbed the upper arm of Reverend Fowler none too gently and marched him toward the front door of the farmhouse, with the rest of his party following closely behind.

As they climbed the steps to the porch, the front door opened and Mrs. Kimball stepped out with an armful of cookware.

"Let me help you with that, ma'am," Joel said as he moved to relieve her of her burden. From her hands he took a heavy pitcher of steaming water and a wide ceramic basin.

"Oh, thank you, Joel. Let me go get you boys some towels and soap now."

Jacob, his fingers still gripping the reverend's arm, watched as Joel set up the basin on the rail of the porch.

The kid grinned at him as he realized what Mrs.

Kimball had brought them. "We have time to wash up before we go, right, Mr. Payne?"

"Yeah, go ahead." It might be the last chance they get at real soap and hot water for a while; they might as well take the extra five minutes to enjoy it.

Mrs. Kimball returned to the porch, carrying further supplies for her guests, with her husband right behind her. Joel busied himself with the water while Jacob handled the visitor.

"My wife tells me—" Mr. Kimball began, stopping when he noticed Reverend Fowler. "What can I do for you, Reverend?" he asked, his voice cold.

Reverend Fowler shook off Jacob's grip and again straightened his jacket. With his arm now free, he removed his hat, nodding politely to Mrs. Kimball before dropping his voice in reverence. "Mr. Kimball, I've come to pray with you. To offer myself as an intercessor with our Lord Jesus Christ, on behalf of your family and your dearly departed Flora."

Mr. Kimball frowned. "Now, my Flora might be dear to me, and she might have temporarily departed this farm, but I don't like your tone. I don't like what you are insinuating."

"I understand it may be difficult to accept," Reverend Fowler said, placing his hand over his heart. "But this is a chance, sir. An opportunity. God has spared your life and granted you more time on earth to accept him as your Lord and Savior and—"

"Hold on now just a minute." Kimball clenched one of his giant, meaty hands into a fist. "My God is the same as your God. You can't come here, come onto *my* land, and tell me I am any less saved than you." He punctuated his sentence by stepping forward, pointing his finger at the reverend and pushing it hard into his chest.

Reverend Fowler stumbled backward a couple steps. Jacob watched, ready to break them apart if necessary. Though Kimball may be in the right, angering and attacking the town preacher was not a step that would serve him.

"Reverend Fowler," Jacob said. "I think maybe this is not the place for you. Why don't you go on back to town and pray from there?"

Kimball glared at his visitor, but kept his lips pursed, guarding himself against saying anything he might regret.

"Wait, wait, wait!" the reverend said, raising his hands above his head. "Wait. If you won't let me pray with you, at least listen to what I have to say."

"Not if it is insulting this good man in his own home," Jacob said.

"No," Reverend Fowler answered, "not that. Though I despair of you recovering the poor girl unharmed and intact, if you are insistent on trying, you should listen to what I have to say."

Jacob exchanged a glance with Kimball. "Why should we listen to you?" he said.

"Believe me." Reverend Fowler placed a hand over his heart again, all but pleading with Jacob. "I have no wish to harm you men, or to let you walk into a situation unprepared. I have had several conversations with this lecherous character Pickens and I believe my knowledge could help you."

"Mr. Payne, the water is getting cold," Joel called

from the end of the porch where he had been getting cleaned up. "You want to come use what's left?"

"Oh heavens," Mrs. Kimball said, bustling over. "Let me warm some more up for you."

"I'd like some of that," Boyd said, crossing to the rail. "If it's not too much trouble, ma'am."

As this small interruption occurred, Jacob took the opportunity to observe Reverend Fowler closer. When he thought no one was looking, when his own attention was trained on the boy and the soapy water, the reverend's expression softened. His shoulders had dropped and his eyes took on a hopeful gleam. In that small moment of unguardedness, Jacob saw what he believed to be the true motivation behind the man's visit.

Reverend Fowler may be pompous and condescending, but he was still a man of God who wanted to help, misguided though he may be.

"All right, Reverend," Jacob said. "Why don't you and me take a seat over here on the steps and you can fill me in on what you learned from Pickens?"

He gestured to the steps at their feet. Reverend Fowler blanched briefly, then bent down to haphazardly dust off the step with his hat and gingerly sat. Jacob stood on the dirt at his feet, put one foot up on the step, and leaned forward on his knee. Zeke leaned on the rail, casually eavesdropping but offering no input. Kimball sat on the other side of the reverend, gun still in hand but staying quiet.

"When did you first meet Pickens?" Jacob began.

Reverend Fowler glanced askance at the muzzle of the gun pointed in his direction. While Jacob himself would never point a gun idly at a neighbor, he noticed that Kimball's hands were nowhere near the trigger and suspected the older man was simply trying to scare the other.

"Well, he, um . . ." Reverend Fowler shot one last glance at Kimball before clearing his throat and directing his answer to Jacob. "Pickens stopped by the rectory not long after he showed up in Elk Springs. The very day he arrived, I think. You may not believe it, but he would not stop talking about that rumored Herron gold mine."

"You don't say?" Zeke answered, rolling his eyes a little.

"It's true," the reverend continued. "He was asking everyone in town if they had heard about the mine. And I believe at least one man pointed the way to this very farm."

"Yes, Reverend," Jacob said with a sigh. "We know all that. Other men in town have already given us those details."

"Did these other men tell you what was in the telegram he sent to Santa Fe?"

Jacob and Kimball exchanged a glance.

"Might as well get to it, Reverend. What do you know?"

He looked at the faces all expectantly watching him and blanched, as though he only just realized the situation he had put himself in.

"Well, as I'm sure is no surprise," Reverend Fowler said pompously, regaining some of his color, "the man is illiterate. He demanded I write down what he wanted the telegram to say, and I have to admit I succumbed to his threats."

"It's fine, Reverend," Jacob said, growing impatient. "We understand why you did it. But what did it *say*?"

"Well, it seems this Pickens character must have accomplices of some sort. He asked his recipient to meet him on this very mountain."

"That means we may be walking into a gang," Boyd said. "What'll we do?"

"Act fast," Jacob said. "We might be able to get to Flora before whoever this accomplice is even arrives. That's plenty to be getting on with. I think it's time we hit the trail."

"Wait, um, Mr. Payne." Joel rushed to his side. "You think maybe we should ask about a horse?"

"A horse?" Mr. Kimball asked, overhearing. "Don't you have a horse?"

"I do, sir." Jacob hesitated. He hated admitting any weakness, even if it was just in his choice of horse. "She is a bit skittish, though. She's borrowed from a friend and I'm not sure—"

"Say no more. I have just the thing."

Jacob followed his host, once again grateful for kind strangers.

CHAPTER EIGHT

Joel led the group of armed men silently down the trail, taking them deeper into the mountains. They had been trekking through the woods for nearly an hour now, with no sign of slowing. The trail was narrow, so small that Jacob was surprised Joel didn't have more trouble following it. He must have spent innumerable hours of his youth exploring this side of the mountain with Flora.

Jacob brought up the rear of their posse, trailing behind Zeke by about twenty feet as he grew accustomed to his new mount. Kimball had been generous enough to loan the bounty hunter one of his stallions. Franny was boarded comfortably in the Kimballs' barn, waiting for Jacob to return. When he had rode off that morning she seemed perfectly happy to be left alone, safe and unmolested.

Instead of a fragile, skittish mare, Jacob's new mount was both mellow and eager to get going. The gorgeous creature's name was Blaze, and though Jacob had only just met him, he was completely at peace with trusting the horse. Indeed, the two seemed to already be experiencing a unique bond. Just the smallest of pressure from Jacob's knees or heels and Blaze obeyed immediately. The horse was at home on the trail and under his new rider.

Jacob was still a little on edge, still worried a tree branch might fall close by and spook his new ride, but told himself he could handle it. Hopefully the stallion was more used to this forest and its sounds than Franny had been, but even if not, he already trusted this horse more. Regardless, Jacob would put up with any obstacles if it meant he was able to get to Flora soon enough.

Up ahead, Jacob heard Joel let out a long, low whistle.

"Mr. Payne?" he called.

Jacob flicked the reins and trotted up along the side of the trail to stand next to Joel. "What did you find?"

Joel had dismounted and was walking slowly a few feet farther along the trail. He didn't even need to answer before Jacob saw what caused him to stop their trek. Ten feet ahead, the dirt trail narrowed even further and passed between rocks. A couple sizable boulders and at least a dozen large stones waited in piles on either side.

Splattered on the rocks, in at least three different places that Jacob could identify from where his horse stood, dark dried blood told the grisly tale of the previous passersby. It wasn't a lot of blood, but it was enough. Whoever spilled this could have a very serious injury and needed their help. If they were still alive.

Joel sniffed. Jacob looked at him sharply, but the young man wasn't facing him. He may be deliberately hiding his tears, but Jacob could guess.

"Let's just remember," Jacob said, "we have no way of knowing if this blood is Flora's. It could be anyone's. It could be an animal's, for all we know. For that matter, we don't even know if it was left recently. Once it's dry, all blood looks the same until it rains."

"I suppose that's true," Joel muttered.

"It rained last week," Boyd offered from behind.

Jacob glared at him. That wasn't helping calm Joel.

"The smartest thing to do," Jacob continued, "is to follow along this trail toward the Herron mine. Same as we were planning. We're like to find more clues along the way, if your guess as to where they're going is right, Joel."

"I never did catch why we're going this way," Zeke said.

"We're going to where the Herron mine is supposed to be."

"Yeah, but . . . it doesn't exist, does it? I heard that dozens of men combed these mountains looking for it and never found a lick of gold."

"No, you're right," Joel said. "It doesn't exist." He rummaged in his saddlebag for a canteen and took a long swig of water before continuing. "I don't know where the initial story came from, but lots of men, and later entire families, came out this way looking for gold. That's how Elk Springs came to be in the first place. A settlement for the gold mine—if there had even been a mine. It's named after the fella that claimed there was a mine here in the first place, sending all those fools out searching in the wilderness. Matthew Herron."

"So then . . ." Boyd removed his hat and scratched his head. "Where are we going?"

"Like I said, I've known the Kimball family since I was about five years old. My father spent a few years looking for the mine and we lived here on the mountain. Flora and me used to play all over their farm, and as we got older we were allowed to venture farther and farther away.

"We had heard all the stories, of course. Growing up in Elk Springs it was like a myth in the back of your mind at all times. 'Look for the Herron mine.' Everyone knew by then that it didn't exist, but they had been in the habit for so long it lingered.

"So, when Flora and I were ten or eleven, we were allowed to venture past the Kimball property line. We spent a lot of time in this forest and on this very trail. We found a cave—it's only a little bit farther up. It's just a cave. It doesn't even go that deep into the mountain, but we started pretending it was the Herron mine. It started out as a joke, but that's what we called it between the two of us.

"Maybe someone else heard us. I know Mr. Kimball called the cave the same thing, but he knew it was just our play spot. Somehow word that Flora knew where the Herron mine is must have gotten out into Elk Springs."

"So that's why we're heading down this trail," Jacob concluded.

"That's right." Joel nodded. "And I hope I'm not wrong. If she's not at this cave, I don't have any other idea where he could have taken her."

"Don't worry, Joel. We'll find her." Jacob believed his own words. "I don't want to assume this is her blood spilled on the mountain, but if nothing else it's a good indication that people came this way."

"I don't understand why she would agree to help him in the first place," Joel said, disappointment and confusion clear on his face. "The Flora I used to know was independent and strong."

"You have to remember, though, that she always felt safe with you, right? If she knows that you're not going to beat her for expressing an opinion, she will be more likely to be herself. But Pickens probably started with violence. She's only seventeen. Does she know how to use a gun?"

Joel shook his head.

"There. You see?" Jacob said. "Going along with the outlaw is just her way of protecting herself. There's not much else she could do if she wanted to stay alive."

"I guess that's so." Joel looked thoughtfully down the trail, farther into the forest where they were headed. "Maybe this blood is a sign she's finally starting to fight back."

"Maybe so," Jacob agreed. "From everything you and your father have said, she seems like a gutsy girl. Let's not worry too much."

Joel nodded. "You're right. Let's keep going."

He mounted his horse again and took the lead, walking slowly down the trail, looking right and left for another clue that Flora and Pickens had passed by this spot. The group stayed quiet. Around them, birds twittered to each other. Every so often one of the horses would huff a deep breath or a small woodland animal would disturb the brush just out of their sight.

If it weren't for the stress of being yet again on the trail of an outlaw, Jacob might have actually enjoyed this ride. The forests of the White Mountains were beautiful. The trail curved up and around to the right, the men climbing farther up the mountain. The air was thinner here than Jacob was used to. Just before the trail curved around again to the left, Joel let out a strangled cry.

He quickly jumped off his horse and tore up the trail.

"What is it?" Jacob asked in a carrying whisper. Since he wasn't sure what Joel had spotted, he didn't know how close the enemy might be. "Joel!"

The young man darted ahead to something just off the side of the trail. He crouched down, hesitated, and then snatched something off the ground. A small scrap of something colorful that Jacob couldn't make out at this distance.

When Joel turned back toward the rest of the group, his face displayed pure fury. His cheeks were flushed, and even from this distance Jacob could see that he was clenching his jaw. The muscles in the boy's neck stood out as he stomped back toward the others.

He held out his hands in front of him, the slip of color now draped across his palms. It was a narrow lavender ribbon, maybe eighteen inches long. As he drew closer, Jacob noticed that one of the ends was frayed and he wondered where the rest of the ribbon had gone.

"It's Flora's," Joel said as he approached. "It's Flora's. I remember when she got this hair ribbon for her birthday. She loved this color. How could she have lost it?"

"Maybe she didn't lose it," Jacob suggested. "Maybe she deliberately dropped it."

In a moment, Joel's entire expression changed from despair to hope. He clenched the ribbon in his fist and smiled at Jacob. "You're right. And maybe this end is frayed because she tried dropping some pieces earlier on the trail and we just missed them."

Jacob nodded encouragingly. "That would be real smart of her."

Joel's eyes shone. "Flora is a smart girl."

Jacob smiled. "So, now we know for sure we're on the right trail."

"Yes!"

"Let's not keep her waiting."

Joel moved quickly, jumping back on his horse and taking the lead again as they continued on the trail toward the cave he and Flora had called the Herron Mine.

They rode more quickly now that they were sure they were on the correct path. The horses carried them up and up the rocky trail, winding around curves of the mountain and between the trees. The sun climbed in the sky and Jacob wondered if they should stop to eat.

Joel held up a hand, pausing their advance.

When Joel paused their advance, Jacob dismounted, tossed the reins to Zeke, and crept up on foot to the young man at the head of their posse.

"What is it?" he whispered, scanning the area.

Joel pointed. "The cave is just past there. Look!"

Jacob followed where the young man indicated. Farther up, the trail continued into the dark, dense forest. For a brief moment he didn't see anything unusual. At a glance, there was no clear reason why Joel had stopped at this spot. The light peeking in through the forest canopy ahead flickered and flashed, making Jacob think he saw movement where there wasn't any.

He sniffed the air, but couldn't make out anything out of the ordinary. Earth, forest, and animal scents all wove around them, but other than Joel on his horse next to him, Jacob didn't smell anything that alluded to Pickens or anyone else being nearby.

But his gut said differently. The bounty hunter

kept his gaze trained down the length of the trail to where Joel had pointed as he crept forward a little farther on foot, darting behind the trunk of a large tree in case whatever Joel had seen was watching back. The longer he looked the more he noticed.

Just through the trees, Jacob noticed the trail about thirty feet ahead curving around an enormous boulder. From this distance he was guessing, but the boulder likely would tower several feet above his own head. It seemed to form a virtual wall of rock presumably continuing past the curve and along the trail farther up the mountain. Small cracks in the boulder revealed the smallest weeds and tiny plants trying to take hold, but the stone seemed nearly impenetrable.

It would be the perfect cover and protection for an outlaw.

Just as he was about to turn back to Joel to ask what he had noticed, movement caught his eye. The flash of a purple skirt wafted into view from behind the boulder before winking out of sight again. There was someone there. Jacob had no doubt he had seen a skirt. There was a woman just out of sight.

He prayed it was Flora Kimball.

Jacob strained his ears to listen. He almost thought he could identify a faint mumble of conversation, but couldn't hear anything more above the horses' heavy breathing and occasional pawing at the ground.

He had to get closer. But he couldn't leave the others behind.

He crept back to Joel and whispered quick instructions, then repeated the same to Boyd and

Zeke. He needed the men to drop anything holding them back so they could be the most nimble on their approach to rescue the girl. The men would find a tree and cover, far off the trail, to leave their horses. Then they could all move forward quietly to inspect what was on the other side of that boulder and hiding farther up the mountain.

Once those steps were underway, Jacob was on his own again. He moved off the path and through the trees, winding his way downhill. His revolver in hand, the bounty hunter kept a focused watch on his prey—or where he hoped he'd find his prey—while he moved to a better position. He took a wide, arching path so he could observe while staying out of sight, downwind, and flank the mysterious camp. As he progressed downhill, winding between the trees, more and more of the scene on the trail became clear. From this angle, it was evident that the boulder had been hiding quite a lot. Joel's eye had been sharp, far sharper than the bounty hunter's.

Jacob spied the remains of a campfire, a pile of saddlebags and two horses tied not far away. But in spite of this evidence of habitation on the trail, he could not actually see any humans. He would have almost thought that he had imagined the purple dress, the site was so quiet. But no. He was sure he had seen it. There must be someone nearby.

Where had she gone?

The boulder itself curved into the side of the mountain, creating a rocky wall that the trail wound around. The rock wall disappeared into a narrow crevice that marked the opening of the cave. It was wider than a man, but not by much. Just a small break in the rock that continued down the length of the trail, forming a wall and cliff on the mountain face.

Joel, Boyd, and Zeke reached him in his hiding spot just downhill from the empty campsite.

"I'm sure I saw movement," Joel insisted in a whisper.

"I did, too," Jacob answered. "They must have gone back in the cave."

"But that was Flora, right? You saw the dress, right? It matched her hair ribbon that I found."

Jacob nodded, keeping his eyes trained on the split in the rock where the cave hid who-knew-what.

If he had been on his own, Jacob might have rushed the group or gone in guns blazing and put himself at risk. Or perhaps he wouldn't have seen the hiding place at all. With Joel, and the other men, he was not only better informed, but also safer. He was warned about the cave, and he had the security of three other gunmen to help him cover the area.

"How deep is that cave, Joel? How many men do you think he could be hiding?"

"Oh, it's big enough for quite a group, but there's only the two horses."

"That's true, but—"

Jacob's planning was interrupted by the sound of yelling coming from up near the campsite. He shut his mouth quickly and ducked down as three figures came stumbling out from the mouth of the cave and into the open campsite.

A blond girl, her hair hanging loosely around her shoulders, her purple calico dress dusty and torn in places, stalked out from the dark crevice, walking backward toward the campsite. Her right hand was held high above her head, and though Jacob couldn't see for sure from this distance, she appeared to be wielding a weapon of some kind. Maybe a rock. On its own, held in her small hand, the rock might not do that much damage, but Jacob had seen how much power and strength a woman could have when she was in danger. He would bet on the girl in this situation any day. After all, she had already figured out how to free herself from whatever binding they'd most likely had her in.

Two men, dirty and rough, stalked out of the cave after her, moving to either side. She was trying to walk backward, away from her pursuers, and kept checking over her shoulder for where she was going to step next. Jacob found himself holding his breath, anxious for her to gain the upper hand. Should he move to help? The two men both had guns trained on her, and a sudden movement from him might cause one of them to pull the trigger.

Flora continued her backward stagger. Trying to look in three different directions would prove difficult for anyone, and, sure enough, she put her foot down in the wrong place, stumbled, and fell into the dirt. The outlaws—one must be Pickens—stalked toward her. Their lecherous grins made Jacob shudder.

"Flora!" Joel cried in a strangled whisper.

Jacob put his hand on the boy's shoulder to keep him from rushing out and revealing their hiding places.

"We'll get her, Joel. But we have to be smart and plan it."

"Now! We have to get her now!"

Jacob nodded, not bothering to try to calm the boy down. If all went according to plan, in just a few moments he could have the girl. It was time to take their shot.

"Stay where you are, son. It won't do Flora any good to have you shot because those despicable men spotted you."

"But—"

"This is our best chance," Jacob said, speaking to Boyd and Zeke. "Joel and I take the one on the left. You two men take the one on the right. If we all shoot at the same time, they won't have a chance to fight back, even if one of us misses."

Jacob had to admit it wasn't the best of plans, but it would do in a pinch.

"Watch out for Flora," Joel said.

"She should be out of the way. She'll be fine. Don't shoot to kill, though. If possible, we need to let the law determine these men's fate. Everyone understand?"

The faces around him all nodded with the same look of grim determination.

"Ready? On my count," Jacob whispered, taking careful aim. "One. Two . . ."

Before he could finish his count, they were interrupted by the sound of hooves galloping toward the camp. Jacob's stomach dropped.

CHAPTER TEN

"Hold your fire," Jacob said to his men.

He lowered his own revolver and darted ahead a few steps to the next wide tree trunk between Flora, the men who held her captive, and himself.

"Damn," he muttered.

They had missed their chance at easily overpowering the villains while there were only two of them. The horses he had heard approaching came around the curve in the trail from the opposite direction—three more dirty, rugged men, riding into camp from the opposite side of the mountain. Jacob could see at a glance that these were not men from Elk Springs. These newcomers had spent the night outside, undoubtedly after having ridden the several hundred miles from Santa Fe. Jacob was glad he wasn't any closer, if not just because he wouldn't want to have to smell those fellas.

But now Jacob and his team were outnumbered. Five to four—not even including the encumbrance of helping Flora get away on top of overpowering her captors. The easy moment had passed him by and now he would have to come up with a better plan.

He needed to get closer. If he could get close enough, Jacob would be able to listen to their plan. The more information he had the easier it would be for him to identify their weaknesses and infiltrate or ambush them.

Jacob looked around. The forest wasn't dense enough for him to be able to get much closer. The trees in the White Mountains were primarily some variation of pine. They were tall and straight, with increasingly smaller branches as they stretched toward the sky. He could dart from tree to tree, but in the spaces between—or even his broad shoulders sticking out around the width of the skinny trunks— he could be found out. He could send Joel, who was thinner and possibly quicker, but he wasn't sure the boy would remember all the details to report back.

He didn't have any other options. Every hesitation put Flora more at risk.

Jacob glanced once more at the five outlaws now congregating around the mouth of the cave. Not one of them even glanced in his direction, so sure were they that they had gotten away with their kidnapping. And for good reason, Jacob thought to himself crossly, though maybe he could use that to his advantage now. He, Joel, and the other two men hadn't even started on the trail for almost two days after Flora had been taken. That would have been plenty long enough to lull Pickens into a feeling of security. Given time, his men to reinforce him, and this cave, of course Pickens was feeling invincible. Of course he wasn't concerned about any rustling noises in the forest around him.

The man's arrogance and obliviousness would be just what led to his demise, Jacob vowed to himself.

He looked back at the other three men and caught Boyd's eye. He held up his hand, indicating that they should wait where they were, then pointed to himself, and farther up the incline. Boyd nodded, his hand on his gun, glancing anxiously between Jacob and the group of ruffians past him.

Jacob was satisfied. The men would remain where they were, but keep an eye on him as he went, providing him cover in case things went wrong.

And he couldn't afford a single thing to go wrong. Not anymore. He had already missed too many chances to rescue the poor girl.

The bounty hunter all but tiptoed through the ground cover and dried pine needles that blanketed the mountain beneath his feet. Three long steps to the next-closest tree trunk large enough to shelter him—most of him, anyway. Once there, he paused to listen for any indication he had been spotted.

Nothing.

A peek around the trunk to check his progress and then four more loping steps to the next wide trunk. The trees were thinning and he had to stand sideways, his right shoulder leaning against the wood, to ensure he stayed hidden. Jacob took off his hat and held it against his chest, worried that the brim might have stuck out and given him away.

He slowed his breath and listened.

"Manage to beat it out of her yet?" one of the men asked.

Jacob heard a shuffle—leather, maybe some metal—and hooves pawing at the ground. He couldn't risk poking his head around the tree this close. The group of outlaws was now only about thirty feet up the slope from him. Judging by the sounds, though, Jacob would guess that the men were busying themselves in making camp. Most likely planning to stick around this spot for awhile.

"No," a second voice answered.

There was a muted *thud* and a tiny whimper that made Jacob think that Flora had been kicked or punched. His temper flared and it took all his patience to keep himself from rushing up the hill, guns blazing. He calmed himself—getting Flora killed in a fire fight wouldn't help anyone.

"She still claims it's not actually a mine," the second voice continued. "I dunno, Morris. Maybe she's telling the truth."

"Maybe. But then, if she is that means we have no more use for her."

Jacob could practically hear the sneer in the man's voice.

"Just let me go," a sweet, feminine voice sobbed. "Let me go home. I showed you where the mine was supposed to be."

"*Supposed* to be," the second voice repeated. By now Jacob guessed that was likely his man, full name Homer Pickens. "But I don't yet see even a flake of gold in my hand, missy. Do you?"

"I don't know how to mine gold!" she cried. Jacob

was gratified to hear some strength and sass come into her voice. The girl had a backbone yet. "I'm just a girl. You think if I knew how to mine gold I'd just leave it in there?"

"She has a point, Homer." A mumbling third man joined the conversation.

Jacob snickered quietly to himself, imagining the scene. The girl had some spunk, he had to give her that.

"Shut up!"

A piercing yelp split the air as Jacob heard the unmistakable sound of a hand slapping flesh.

"My lip!" she cried. "I'm bleeding!"

Jacob felt another wave of fury, this one dwarfing the last, rolling over him. Robbing banks or rustling cattle was one thing. Though he didn't agree with it, Jacob understood what might drive a man to that kind of activity. But laying a hand on a woman? Assaulting a delicate creature? Not to mention doing all this to her while she's tied up and unable to even run away from such violence.

No, these men would pay. There was no excusing that behavior.

This would take some strategy, he reminded himself. He and his small posse would need thoughtful planning to take them by surprise or to sneak in to rescue the girl.

Jacob retreated back to where the others were waiting. He shook his head in answer to Joel's questioning look.

"We can't stay here," he said. "We—"

"I'm not leaving her!" Joel hissed. "You go back, if you must. I'm going to find a way to rescue Flora."

"Joel, I'm not going back to Elk Springs. Keep your voice down. We just can't stay in this spot. It's too exposed. Let's go back to the horses and reassess."

Joel looked like he wanted to protest. He kept glancing back to where Flora had disappeared down the dark mouth of the cave and wasn't moving his feet. Jacob firmly wrapped his fingers around the boy's upper arm and dragged him away.

Jacob dragged the boy away from the mouth of the cave and led the group around the curve of the mountain, between the trees, traveling as quietly as they could to not draw attention to themselves. Jacob had a feeling that the men would be distracted for quite a while—what with looking for gold, fighting among themselves, and keeping Flora in line—but it still behooved him to be cautious.

When they had reached the trail again, now on the other side of the boulder, Boyd took the lead back to where their four horses had been tied.

"We've got to go back," Joel insisted with a hiss.

Jacob unbuckled the leather cover of the pack on Blaze and pulled out a side of jerky. He tossed a piece to Joel and took a bite himself, chewing slowly while he thought out the next steps.

"We will go back, son," he said patiently. "But you saw those men. Five of them. With cave cover, to boot. Now that we know more of their plan, we can take advantage of it."

"What's their plan?" Zeke asked.

Jacob explained what he had overheard about the mine and how they thought they needed Flora.

"That's ridiculous," Joel said. "There has never been a mine there."

"I know that. You know that. *Flora* knows that, and said as much repeatedly to her thick-headed kidnappers. Seems they don't want to believe it."

"But what are they going to do to Flora while they're trying to find the gold?"

Jacob shook his head. He didn't want to put it into words.

"What will they do when they finally accept that she can't help them?"

Jacob just shook his head again.

Joel grabbed Jacob's arm, pulling on him, starting to panic.

"Here's what I'm thinking," Jacob said, not answering Joel directly. "They look like they'll be going in and out of the cave, since they set up camp outside. Which means that at some point, not all five of them will be together. One or two of them will be isolated if we watch carefully enough. We just need to wait for the right moment, overpower the one or two that remain outside and take it from there."

Boyd nodded. "Yeah. I think that could work."

"But we have to time it exactly," Jacob emphasized. "Too late or too early and we could find all five of those madmen swarming down on us."

"Do you know who they are?" This from Zeke.

Jacob shook his head. "No, I don't, none except Homer Pickens. Which means I'd rather we don't kill them if we don't have to. I always want to take them alive if possible, but more so now while we don't even know their identities. Standing by idly while a girl is held hostage is not admirable, certainly, but it's also not a crime worthy of death."

Joel grumbled under his breath about this last part, but Jacob chose to ignore it. The kid was under a lot of pressure and had likely never been in such high stakes before.

"Let's not have any confusion," he said. "I will decide when the right moment is. You all will follow my cue, my lead, and my instructions. If I detect any mutiny among you"—he pointed to each man in turn —"I will turn my considerable skill to subduing you first. Believe me when I tell you I am more than capable of taking all three of you on if I have to." He said this last directly to Joel.

"Got it, boss," Boyd said, answering for the others.

Jacob kept his gaze on Joel, and the young man finally nodded.

"All right. Follow me."

He led the group of men through the trees, back toward the outlaws' campsite, then back around the other side of it. Jacob cut his own path through the trees to the right and uphill of the boulder, up over where the cave entrance cut into the mountain. The slope of the mountain grew steep as the four made their way back to the cave. The overhang was bare of trees, and even the low shrubs were sparse.

"Leave your hats," Jacob instructed in a whisper.

They left a pile at the foot of one of the pine trees and crawled forward on their bellies. Elbows pulling them forward along the dirt, the men stayed as silent as possible. From behind him, Jacob heard Zeke blow out air through pursed lips, likely pushing a weed or spider web out of his face.

They slowly, carefully approached the edge, knowing that just below them, only ten feet away, were five men who could easily kill them as soon as they saw them. Jacob gestured the men forward, so all four were lying low to the ground in a row, looking over the edge to the campsite.

Now all they had to do was wait for the right moment. Once there was but a single outlaw outside the cave, Jacob would simply jump down the few feet to the ground below and take him prisoner.

It should be easy. It would just take time.

At the moment, four of the five men, plus the girl, were sitting in the dirt around the campsite. One of the men was roasting something over the embers and the others were fiddling with their various weapons or tools. To Jacob's eyes it seemed like they were all just wasting time, waiting for something.

One of the men's voices floated up to them. "I didn't ride all the way out here from Santa Fe for no gold, Pickens. If Jack can't find nothing down there you'll be compensating me by other means."

"Oh shut up, Morris," Pickens answered from across the campsite. "You've traveled farther for far less. That whore of yours in New Orleans ain't worth half what you can get here."

"And yet I still got nothin' in my hand."

"The gold is in there. Four different people told me this here girl knew where the mine is."

"Sure don't look that way to me. Looks like we been lied to. Are you a fool, Pickens, a fool who believes little girls?"

"Let's see what little Flora has to say." Pickens stood up and crossed the space in two steps to leer over her.

"That's Miss Kimball to you," she said, her voice pure venom.

Such courage was rewarded with a hard slap across the face. Jacob winced when he heard the crack, but silently cheered the girl for standing her ground.

"Don't you talk back to me, girl."

There was a beat of silence, Flora's head hung down, recovering from the blow. When she looked back up at Pickens, Jacob could see that something in her had broken. She no longer cared to keep her captors happy or to even ensure her own safety. Brow furrowed, she glared at the outlaw with fury, holding his gaze directly. Without breaking eye contact she lifted both feet up. With her ankles still bound she had less leverage, but she still managed to slam the full strength of her legs into the man's knee.

Jacob thought he heard something go *crack*. Pickens collapsed to the dirt.

Two of the other men hurried forward to subdue the girl, yelling and cursing at her, but Pickens stopped them.

"She's mine," he said darkly, holding his hand up to hold them back.

Flora whimpered as she watched Pickens climb painfully to his feet.

"No," she whispered.

He limped toward her, bearing down, looming over her. Flora scooted backward in the dirt, moving awkwardly with her hands bound behind her back, her feet still bound at the ankles. She moved away in this fashion until her back hit the enormous boulder, knocking her head in the surprise. Pickens reached her easily, grabbing one ankle and pulling her violently toward him. He grabbed the skirt of her dress in both hands and ripped it roughly all the way from her hem to her waist.

"No!" Flora cried, sounding truly terrified for the first time.

CHAPTER TWELVE

"No!" Joel cried.

"Shhh. Joel. You have to keep your voice—"

"No, I won't. They can't do that to her. I can't let them!"

"Joel, you've got to—"

Zeke reached up and wrapped his arms around Joel's leg. The kid tried to kick him off, but Zeke managed to hang on, wrestling the kid to the ground and at least temporarily stopping him from giving away their position. But the twenty-year-old was too strong, too wiry. He struggled and pulled and slipped out of the older man's grasp.

Jacob tried again to calm the kid down, but Joel was inconsolable. And he was strong. He easily shook off Jacob's hands as he climbed to his feet.

"She needs me!" he cried, jumping down to the campsite below.

Jacob ducked his head, praying that the other men would think to do the same. They had to hide from view, for when the outlaws would inevitably look up to where the boy had come from.

"Joel Colfax!" Flora cried in amazement.

Jacob put out his hands, stopping Boyd and Zeke from going after Joel. There was no sense in all of them putting themselves in danger. If he was careful there might still be a way to salvage this. If Joel would just . . .

Jacob and the other two men listened helplessly. There was no response from the kid. With his head down and hidden, Jacob could only hear what was happening. He would have to guess. There were several heavy thuds that sounded like punches to his gut or back, along with a *crack!* that certainly marked a hit to the boy's head.

"Joel," cried Flora, subdued.

Jacob shook his head to himself. Even without seeing what was happening, it was clear that whatever men had been outside the cave when the kid jumped down were plenty to trounce him.

"Lord God in Heaven," Boyd said under his breath.

"Dammit!" Jacob scrunched up his face, closing his eyes against the reality of his new situation. With Joel now captured, their entire balance of power was in doubt. "Damn," he whispered again.

He gestured to the other two men to get their attention. When they looked at him, Jacob pointed back down the mountain and began to crawl backward, out of sight and out of hearing of the outlaws below. Satisfied that he heard the other men following him, he continued his climb.

He had to start over with a new plan. Again.

Once he was a sufficient distance away, Jacob got to his feet, dusted the dirt off his front, and strode another dozen feet into the forest for better cover.

Zeke and Boyd were close behind him. Their searching looks reminded Jacob of how little his team was prepared for this kind of stand-off. These two men had likely never dealt with outlaws of Pickens's ilk and were looking to Jacob to show them how it was done.

"Well . . ." Jacob began slowly. He took a deep breath and let it out as quietly as he could. "This complicates things."

"We can't . . . you're not serious?" Boyd said fearfully.

"What? That it'll be difficult to get Flora *and* Joel back? Why the hell do you think we're even here, Boyd?"

"Just us three against them five? I dunno, Jacob. We had a chance when there was just two of them. We mighta could done something with Joel still with us. But now? I just don't see how we're going to free them kids."

"There must be a way," Jacob insisted. "There's always a way."

"No. Huh-uh." Boyd shook his head. "It's over."

"Yeah, Boyd's right," Zeke said, nodding grimly. "We all got families. We can't be putting ourselves at risk any more than we already have. My wife is expecting me home. You gonna be the one to tell her I got shot trying to rescue some stranger?"

"Let me ask you something, Mr. Boyer. You got a daughter?"

Zeke nodded.

"A son?"

"Three boys and a girl." He stood up a little straighter and puffed up his chest with pride. Jacob noted the shine in his eyes when he mentioned his kids. This was a man who cherished his family and was proud of them. A man who valued his home life. The kind of man on whom America was built.

"And"—Jacob lowered his voice even more and leaned forward—"what would you do if one of those children was taken from you? Like Flora has been taken from her own father, and now Joel from his?"

Zeke swallowed hard and looked down at the dirt under his feet.

"Those helpless young ones in that cave are just as loved and just as precious as your own. Do you want to be the one to go home to Mr. Kimball and tell him we gave up? Will you go back with me to Cork to tell Mrs. Colfax we left her son with five of the worst men to grace this part of the country?"

Zeke looked up at his brother-in-law and the two seemed to have a silent conversation about their options. A shrug of a shoulder, a twitch of the lip, and the two men came to a decision.

"All right," Zeke said, nodding. "We'll stay."

Jacob was a little surprised at how easily he'd swung from one decision to another, but he didn't want to question it too hard for fear of changing the man's mind again.

"Okay, then. I still think the original plan is our

best bet," Jacob said. "We can wait till one of those fellas is outside the cave and the others are inside, and take them out one at a time."

"Like an ambush?" Boyd asked.

"Exactly. As long as we stay out of sight from the mouth of the cave we should be just fine."

"They'll never guess what's coming," Zeke said, grinning now that he'd committed himself again—perhaps more so than before. "They're just grimy criminals. There's no way they will be able to beat us."

"Zeke," Jacob said seriously. "We can't underestimate these people. There's a reason they're still free and not rotting in a jail cell somewhere. We have to be smart about this."

"All right, then, what are we waiting for? Let's get to it so we can get home."

"Patience," Jacob said in a carrying whisper. But Zeke was already moving ahead and may not have heard him.

The three crept down the trail back toward where the enormous boulder would block the outlaws' view of their approach. Jacob strained to listen, to get a sense of what was going on just out of his view. It seemed too quiet to have more than maybe a couple of the outlaws outside the cave, but Jacob could smell the campfire burning down to embers.

"I don't hear anything," Zeke said excitedly. "We can get them now! The next one that comes outta there is gonna get a bullet in the side."

He strode on ahead, ignoring Jacob's hissing commands to wait and be careful. Zeke was making too much noise. Jacob couldn't reach him to pull him back before the other man popped his head and shoulders around the corner of the large stone wall. He moved into view of whoever might be at the campsite before he even had his pistol ready.

"Zeke!" Jacob whispered, desperate not to blow their cover.

A gunshot tore through the quiet.

Jacob started forward to help Zeke, but he was too slow. The man cried out, first in pain from the bullet piercing his upper arm, and then again from the pain of being seized and manhandled by the two outlaws who had been on guard.

"Who the hell is this?" one of the men asked angrily. "Where did you come from? You meddling sons-a-b—"

"Who else is out there?" the other man asked.

Jacob held his breath and backed away from the trail. He held Boyd back, flat against the boulder, watching as the grimy outlaw strode out from cover and into view. He looked right and left; he peered into the forest in front of him. With the hard afternoon light, the shadows between the trees were dark and distinct, hiding movement. As long as the man didn't come around to their side of the boulder, Jacob and Boyd would be safe.

Jacob readied his revolver, holding it steady, and aimed at the curve around which the outlaw might come.

After a few seconds of searching, the man returned back to the campsite, out of Jacob's line of sight.

"Grab that one," the voice commanded on the

other side of the boulder. "If he's come after these two, there's more to their story than they're telling us."

"What are we doing with them? What if there's more of 'em?"

"Let's take 'em down to the depths of the mine. Maybe being down the shaft will jog their memory."

Jacob heard a series of pained cries as Flora, Joel, and Zeke were seized and likely dragged down into the dark, narrow cave. He could smell the fire outside the mouth of the entrance still burning, but try as he might he couldn't hear any human. The several pairs of footsteps faded away down the path and Jacob and Boyd were left alone.

"How can we get them now?" Boyd asked in a panicked whisper. "We have to go back to town. Get more men."

Jacob shook his head. There was still a way to do this. He just had to outthink the gang leader and stay one step ahead. They had to be quick about it, though. Before Zeke bled out. Before the men realized that Flora and Joel couldn't help them. With every moment that slipped by, the chance of getting all of their group safely back to Elk Springs grew smaller and smaller.

He and Boyd retreated to consider their options and make a plan.

"Jacob, we need to go back. We need to get help. We can't do this. There's too many of them. And too few of us. We can't. Jacob, we can't!"

"Come on now, Boyd," Jacob said soothingly. "Calm down now. If we take the time to go all the way back to town, who knows what will happen to them. Zeke's bleeding with every second we waste."

"Yeah, but—"

"It's too far. That's too much time. We have to figure this out on our own. Here. Now."

"Jacob, I don't know . . ."

"Do you want to go, then?"

Jacob gave the man a hard look. He needed to know if he was alone in this, if he would have to concoct a plan that was him against the entire outlaw gang, if he had any other kind of help on his side. Boyd swallowed under Jacob's gaze and looked down at his feet.

"I guess . . . I . . . yeah, okay. You're right. My sister will skin me alive if I come home without Zeke."

Working as quickly and quietly as they could, Jacob and Boyd spent the next fifteen minutes finalizing the plan for what would hopefully be their final assault. With all the tools they needed in hand, Jacob and Boyd headed back down the trail toward the cave for one final attempt at rescuing the captives.

It felt as though he was repeating himself—tentative attack only to be taken down before he even started. If this plan didn't work, Jacob despaired of ever rescuing the other three. He already worried about the innocent girl being in their clutches for too long, and what had happened to her in all the time Jacob couldn't see.

But he squared his shoulders and readied himself for the battle ahead.

Jacob cautiously rounded the corner, hugging the boulder with his back, and approached the mouth of the cave. With the heat of the afternoon, the group of outlaws had retreated into the cool of the cave. Sounds of their shouts, pickaxes, clanging, and arguing came echoing out of the narrow hole in the ground.

After he and Boyd had properly set up their plan, Jacob stepped to the opening of the cave and shouted:

"We've come to claim the bounty!"

Jacob stood in the mouth of the cave, knowing that he could be targeted and shot with no effort from his enemy. His entire frame would be backlit, his silhouette providing the exact target for the outlaws in the cave below.

"Bring out the outlaws—Flora Kimball and Joe Colfax," Jacob shouted again. "We'll be claiming their bounties. You have no right to them."

Boyd stood off to the side of the cave, shaking the trembles from his hands, as Jacob called for the dangerous men to show themselves.

"Stay out of sight," Jacob reminded him.

Deep down in the darkness of the cave, he heard the outlaws muttering to each other, probably debating the next step. It was always to Jacob's advantage when he came across a group with no clear leader. Their infighting would work in his favor.

"Go to hell!" a deep voice shouted up at him.

"I'm here for the three I know you have," Jacob

yelled. "There's no use protecting them. They need to meet their justice."

More muttering and heated discussions floated up from the cave. Jacob pressed on loudly.

"The girl may have tricked you into thinking she's innocent, but the law says otherwise."

"If there's a bounty, we'll be the ones collecting," a voice shouted back to Jacob.

He grinned to himself. "Maybe we can come to some sort of agreement. I'd be happy to discuss it peaceably in the light of day."

He held both of his hands out, so by his silhouette it was clear he was not holding any weapons. If he could draw at least one of them out . . .

Before he had even finished the thought, Jacob heard footsteps echoing off the rock walls, getting ever louder as one of the men stalked out of the cave toward him. As he moved into the light, Jacob saw that he was the tall, bullying man the others had called Morris.

"Let's see those hands," Jacob said. "I'm not armed, and I don't want to negotiate with a man who is."

"Who said anything about negotiating?" the man asked with a snarl. He pointed his shotgun at Jacob, who kept his hands in the air. "You're gonna give us the details of that bounty. And then we're gonna leave here with the prisoners. Shoulda thought about that before you opened your big mouth."

"Wait, now." Jacob kept his hands in the air, signaling his innocence, but took a small step toward the man. Behind him, Boyd waited, eyes huge and fearful but still ready to play his part. "We can talk about this. How're y'all going to move three outlaws without horses?"

The other man's face grew dark. "What did you do with our horses?"

In a panic he turned to follow the trail to where their horses had been corralled, but Boyd was ready. Before the tall man had even finished his pivot, the other had swung down and hard with a shovel he had swiped from the outlaws' stash. The direct hit knocked the man unconscious immediately.

Morris collapsed into Boyd's arms and was dragged away. Jacob did his best to disguise the silhouette of this interaction from whoever might be watching below, but now his window of opportunity was closing even faster.

"Morris?" a voice called up from below. "Where'd you go?"

"Your friend went to go check on the horses, since you have such a ride ahead of you."

Jacob glanced off to the side of the trail, pleased to see Boyd had already tied and gagged their first man. Cattle-rassling fast.

"Come on out, now. Bring the hostages with you. Their bounty will feed us for months."

After a beat of silence, the same voice called up again. "Where's Morris?"

Jacob glanced over. The man was still unconscious, Boyd grinning over him.

"He's busy. I told you. There's no point staying here any longer. By now you probably have figured out that this ain't a real gold mine, right?"

"Wait. How did you . . . ?"

"That's their scam." Jacob took a step farther into the cave. "That trio has bilked half a dozen people out of finder's fees and false maps by claiming they knew the way to a secret gold mine or silver mine. How much did the girl's story cost you?"

"Well, actually, we—"

Another voice: "Shut up!"

Jacob grinned to himself, imagining the men fighting down below, not paying attention, giving him a little more ground to press his advantage.

"That's why there's such a big bounty out for them." Jacob continued, pretending he hadn't heard their arguing. "And why I don't intend to leave this mountain without them."

There was one last pause before they shouted to him again.

"Go to hell! We're not giving anything up. Especially not if you have Morris."

"All right, then. I tried reasoning with you. I tried being nice. No more. You have ten seconds to come up out of there before I blow you out."

"Bull!"

"Let us go!" Flora cried.

Jacob felt a twinge of guilt. She didn't know him. She hadn't met him. And it was unlikely that either Zeke or Joel had had a chance to talk to her privately. For all the poor girl knew, he was just as dangerous as the men who currently held her captive. Out of the frying pan, into the fire.

"Are you going to save yourself and those bounties you have tied up?" Jacob asked. "If you don't die immediately from the explosion, you're sentencing yourself to a long starvation or suffocation from the cave-in. Best come out now."

"I'm calling your bluff," Pickens said. "There's no way this girl is any kind of criminal."

Jacob took a deep breath, considering his next move. But he was out of maneuvers. This was the last thing he could do before he would either have to admit defeat for the first time or risk getting everyone killed.

He laughed. "Your funeral. Ten . . . nine . . . eight . . ."

As he counted down loudly, he moved to the side of the trail where, earlier, he'd planted the prop. It had to be convincing and it had to be ready in advance, in case negotiations had gotten to this step.

". . . five . . . four . . ."

Jacob turned his back to the mouth of the cave so the men inside were blocked from seeing what he did. The bundle of dried branches was bound tightly. It was small and narrow, as close to the dimensions of a stick of dynamite that Jacob could manage. With one longer branch sticking out of one end, in silhouette it resembled dynamite so closely that Jacob was the only one who should be able to tell the difference.

". . . two . . . one!"

Jacob held the end of the bundle over the still-smoldering campfire, waited for the spark to catch, and then tossed the smoking decoy down into the dark cave.

"Here it comes!" he shouted.

With every dangerous criminal that Jacob Payne hunted down, there would always be a small moment, a breath of time when he doubted himself, when the plan could collapse. A moment when he could fail. Immediately after he tossed the smoking bundle down into the cave, Jacob closed his eyes tightly and clenched his fists. That brief second to say a desperate prayer calmed his nerves.

He opened his eyes when he heard the yelps and cursing coming from the darkness. Jacob walked a few steps down into the mouth of the cave, closer to where his homemade smoke decoy was burning and hopefully forcing the outlaws out. Behind him, Boyd stood ready and waiting silently. The forest filled with the commotion, shuffling, and yelling as the sounds of his enemies bounced off the rock walls.

"Leave them!" one of the men yelled. "They're not worth it!"

"No!" Flora cried.

"Let us go!" Joel yelled.

It must be chaos down there, Jacob thought. He didn't know what kind of lantern or light source they had been working with, but as he couldn't see anything in the corridor ahead, it must not be much.

"Are they coming?" Boyd whispered.

Jacob nodded, drawing his gun. They would only have one chance to overpower the men as they exited the cave. He stepped backward back into the afternoon light.

"Come on!" one of the men shouted, getting closer.

Time slowed as the enemy approached.

When he was putting together the decoy dynamite, Jacob had thought carefully about how he could quickly capture five armed men, with only himself and Boyd to man the weapons. He could easily tie up one, probably two of the men on his own, but that left three for the inexperienced local to handle, and they couldn't depend on Joel or Zeke being able to help when the time came. There was no question that Jacob would need to be creative with this step in his plan.

He had thought about it, weighed his options, and considered what assets he had at his disposal. Once he took a wider view of the whole situation, Jacob realized he had much more to work with than just the one man at his side.

Now, as he waited on edge for the four remaining dangerous outlaws to all exit the cave, Jacob stepped back to the side, his back against the boulder wall, squatted down, and picked up the end of the rope that he had previously left lying there in the dirt. The length of the rope was limp on the ground, across the mouth of the cave, until it curved up, the other end was securely tied to the saddle of his horse, Blaze.

The strength and control of that mustang was an ace up his sleeve that Jacob had completely forgotten he'd had. He supposed he'd gotten too used to the absence of Paint—especially after having to disregard Franny entirely. He was newly encouraged when he remembered that Blaze, or maybe the other horses, could be brought in to help.

As the men poured out of the cave, Jacob pulled up his end of the rope. Pickens and his cohorts were too frantic and panicked to be paying close-enough attention, and the low rope tripped every single one of them. They fell, one after another getting caught, ankles twisting, knees buckling. The fourth one out of the cave fell fastest, over his own feet and into the back of Pickens. One man grabbed at another to hold him up, and they ended up with elbows and arms enmeshed, crashing to the ground. One after another, the men fell over each other into a tangled mess in the dirt.

Jacob and Boyd lost no time in pushing their advantage.

The shortest of the men scrambled to his feet first, but fumbled in drawing his weapon. Boyd rushed forward with a large stone in one hand and his pistol in the other. Pickens, sprawled in the dirt, grabbed for Boyd's feet as he passed, tripping him. But Boyd kept his feet under him and reached the short man. He swung down, hard and fast, smashing his stone into the side of the man's head and incapacitating him. The man crumpled on the ground and Boyd turned to take on another.

While Boyd was taking care of that man, Jacob grabbed the end of the rope. Leaving it still tied to Blaze's saddle, he wrapped his end three times quickly around the outlaw with the big black beard before he was able to climb to his feet. The man kicked out at Jacob and spat at him.

"You son of a—!"

Jacob kicked the man in the ribs, knocking the wind out of him before he could finish his angry cursing. He pulled a sweaty handkerchief out of his pocket and stuffed it in the man's mouth, further silencing him.

As he finished tying the knot, Jacob heard a *crack* behind him and in front of him almost simultaneously and looked around the space. Pickens had climbed to his feet and pulled his weapon, turning it on Jacob and firing. Whether because of his aim or because of Jacob's movement, the shot missed, hitting the stone wall behind him and breaking a chunk off the boulder.

Pickens saw that Jacob had noticed where the bullet came from and grinned at him. With two teeth missing on the right side of his mouth, the man looked manic. Jacob was a quick draw, but had not yet had a chance to pull his revolver when Pickens collapsed into the dirt. As he crumpled, Boyd's form with a now-bloody stone held in one hand loomed behind.

The fourth and final outlaw had not even stuck around to try to fight it out. He had taken longer to get to his feet, but now was racing as fast as he could down the mountain, off the trail and toward the woods where Jacob had watched their group before. The outlaw must have been injured in his fall; he seemed to be cautious about putting weight on his right foot.

Jacob hesitated only a moment before darting off after him. The man was still close enough that he could have gotten off a clean shot and stopped his progress. Instead, Jacob bounded off down the mountain, catching up with the man in seconds and tackling him to the ground.

The outlaw fought back, kicking, punching, and trying to bite Jacob when his arm got close enough. They tussled in the dirt for a tense ten seconds before Jacob's muscular legs gave him the advantage. He had the other man pinned in the dirt, each of Jacob's legs pinning an arm down, and the outlaw squirmed underneath.

"You want to give up now?" Jacob asked. "Make this easy on yourself? Or do I have to knock you out?"

"You best kill me," the man hissed.

Jacob smirked. "Oh no, my friend. I won't be denying the law their due."

He pulled his fist back, kneeling hard on the man's arms to hold him in place, and swung. Jacob's knuckles connected directly with the man's jaw, just below his ear, knocking him unconscious and leaving him limp in the dirt.

Jacob let out a long, slow breath. Against all odds, they had managed to subdue five outlaws without killing any of them. Jacob had to keep reminding himself that one of these days he would have no choice, that he would have to kill a fugitive to protect himself or someone else. But he was grateful today was not that day.

Fortunately the man was not all that large. Even with his dead weight, Jacob was able to heft him over his shoulder and carry him back up the incline toward the campsite and the others.

The unconscious outlaw dumped alongside the first, Jacob crossed the dirt campsite to where Pickens lay collapsed. There was a tiny rivulet of blood trailing down the back of his head into the dirt, but when Jacob looked closely and probed a bit with his fingers, he decided the cut was shallow and the man would be fine.

Jacob lifted the man to his feet, holding him upright under the armpits. As he was unconscious, the dead weight was difficult to maneuver, but with Boyd's help he managed to get the man up onto the horse, tied and fixed in place.

One by one each of the incapacitated outlaws was trussed up and planted on top of a horse. Jacob had lied, of course—the outlaws' horses were here the whole time.

Jacob surveyed his and Boyd's handiwork, satisfied. Each of these men was complicit in a kidnapping at the very least. But Jacob knew the type—it was likely they were involved in deeper, more dangerous plots. He would take them all back to Elk Springs and let Sheriff Dale deal with them. They could be installed safely in the town jail while wires went out to other towns in the area once they were up and running again.

Once the group of men were subdued securely, it only took a few minutes to hike down into the cave, untie Joel, Zeke, and Flora, and make the necessary explanations. The poor prisoners had had a few petrifying moments, of course, waiting for the "dynamite" to blow up and end them, but they'd soon realized that the burning and smoke was coming from something other than explosive.

"And then once we realized it was just a decoy, it just became a matter of staying out of your way until the rest of your plan had unfolded," Zeke concluded.

Flora was eager to get home, and they still had just enough light left in the day to make it back to her family's farm. Joel led the entire caravan back down the mountain trail.

They had left Flora untethered to a criminal. She had protested, insisting she could do her part to guard them, until Jacob pointed out that she was unarmed. Being free of that burden, Flora rode up at the front of the caravan, side by side with Joel. Jacob was too far back to hear what they said to each other, but the grins they traded back and forth said plenty.

Just as dusk began to settle, Joel led them through the gap in the fence on the backside of the Kimball farm. Flora trotted on ahead, eager to see her family again.

Once Jacob, Boyd, and Zeke had secured their prisoners and their horses by the fence at the front of the property, Jacob approached where Joel was talking to Kimball out on the front porch.

"Sir? Mr. Kimball? I'd . . ." Joel looked at Flora with an expression of worship. "I'd like to marry your daughter."

"I know he's not of our faith, Father," Flora said quickly, "but he's a good man and he loves me and I'm not sure, now, that—"

"Hush, child," Kimball said gently, putting his large, rough hand on his daughter's cheek. "You don't have to explain anything to me. Your mother and I had despaired of ever finding a man of our Heavenly Father worthy of you, anyway. And now, with this whole adventure and the way people talk, I thought . . ." He trailed off and grew quiet.

Joel reached over and clasped Flora's hand. They presented a united front to her father, both wanting nothing more than to just be together, no matter what other circumstances may have led to it.

"I can't promise you it will be easy," Kimball said to them, coming out of his reverie. "The folks in this town have mighty strong opinions about us already, Flora. And now they have an opportunity to question your honor. Marrying Joel won't stop their wagging tongues."

"I know, Father. But I wanted to be his wife a week ago, and even more so now. Please say we have your blessing."

There was another long pause as Kimball looked over the pair. Finally he addressed his proclamation to Joel.

"Son," he said, offering his hand. "You've begun this marriage protecting my daughter at risk of your own life. I expect you to continue the same level of love and protection for the rest of it."

"Yes, sir. Of course, sir. I'm happy to." Joel shook his new father-in-law's hand vigorously, unable to keep the wide grin from his face. "Can we get married today?"

Kimball chuckled. "Your mother would kill me if I let you get married without her being here. We'll send them word. I promise it will be soon."

Jacob wasn't sure the boy had heard, though. He had already turned to his bride-to-be and taken her in his arms. Jacob tried not to watch, to give them a little privacy. But it was clear from what he did see that Joel and Flora would never be happier with anyone else. This was as sure an example of everything working together for good as Jacob would ever see.

The two lovebirds soon hurried into the house. Flora had been wearing the same dress for several days, and they both needed something more substantial in their stomach than simply jerky.

"I'll see to it that word is sent to his parents on my way back through Elk Springs," Jacob promised. "Assuming the wire is fixed by now."

"I appreciate that," Kimball said. "Joel's parents were our closest friends when they lived here, and though I wish the circumstances could be different, I'm sure those two will make a happy couple."

"You ready to go back to town now?" Zeke asked, walking up.

Jacob looked up to where Boyd was standing guard over their prisoners. Each of the five men wore an expression of anger and disappointment. Whatever big plans they had had for the rumored Herron Gold Mine, they'd have to rethink that completely.

"That reminds me," Kimball said, following Jacob's gaze. "While you were gone Reverend Fowler came back with news from Tucson. Homer Pickens is wanted for bank robbery. There's a bounty of three hundred dollars on his head."

Zeke let out a low whistle. "Three hundred? Must have been some robbery."

Kimball continued. "And judging from the descriptions the reverend gave me, I would bet these others you've captured are members of the Slippery Stone Gang that has been roaming these mountains."

"I thought that gang was up in Prescott," Jacob said.

"Some are." Kimball nodded. "But Stone likes to keep lawmen on their toes. He has so many men willing to kill and rob for him that he can split them up for different jobs."

"Well, ain't that a pleasant thought," Jacob said darkly.

"Exactly," Kimball agreed. "But that does mean that there's probably a bounty on those men, too. They could have been anywhere in the Arizona Territory wreaking havoc. You all should be sure to check in with the sheriff and see what can be salvaged from this adventure."

Excitement was dawning on Zeke's face. He looked back at Boyd, who remained focused, his revolver pointed at the prisoners.

"A few hundred dollars split between us is good money," Zeke said. "We're ready as soon as you are, Jacob."

"You boys go ahead," Jacob told him. He walked to the horses alongside Zeke. "We didn't know there would be a bounty when we set off, and I know you all risked more than I did. You take these men back to town and the sheriff will see to your reward. Any man who would risk so much for a neighbor in face of such adversity deserves whatever the world will gift him."

Boyd and Zeke exchanged a glance before nodding, accepting what Jacob had offered them.

"Thank you kindly, Jacob," Zeke said, offering a

shake with his uninjured arm. "We appreciate what you've done for Elk Springs and for both of us. A good man like you doesn't come along all the time, but know that you're always welcome here."

"I know my Sarah would be happy to host you any time," Boyd added.

"I appreciate that. I really do. Next time I'm on this side of the territory I'll take you up on it."

"All right, then," Zeke said as he mounted his horse. "We'll be seeing you, Jacob."

Both men tipped their hats and began the ride back to Elk Springs, a line of five tied outlaws riding between them.

"I couldn't help overhearing," Kimball said, as Jacob turned back toward the farmhouse. "That's very generous of you to let those men claim the reward when you did so much of the work."

Jacob shrugged. "There will be more rewards. This was supposed to be a break from that work, anyway."

Kimball chuckled. "Guess it didn't work out the way you planned."

"No, sir, it didn't."

"What do you think you'll do now?"

Jacob shrugged again. "The horse I'm riding is just a loan. I've got to take Franny back to her owner soon, so I guess I'll just make my way back to Tucson now. There's bound to be a new report ready."

"Those outlaws never stop."

"No, they don't."

Jacob was about to head into the barn to get Franny saddled and ready to head back down the mountain, when Kimball stopped him.

"I've been thinking. The whole time you were gone, putting yourself at risk for my daughter, I was wondering what I could do to ever repay you."

"There's no need—"

"Hush, now." Kimball fixed him with a hard stare. "There is a need. Flora is dearer to me than you may realize. With her blessed mother gone, and us moved all the way out to Arizona, Flora and Edith are the only things left that are around to remind me of the love of my youth. When you went after her, I was left with hours imagining what I would do if you didn't succeed."

Jacob listened respectfully, thinking of his own memory of his marriage, and the little he had left of his late wife.

"There is nothing that can make up for what you've given back to me, but I thought maybe you'd accept a small gift of my appreciation."

Jacob smiled. "I will, sir. Something small I can take with me back to Tucson would be kind and much appreciated."

"Wonderful." Kimball beamed. "I hoped you'd say that. Come with me."

Jacob moved to follow the older man into the house, but instead he turned the opposite direction to lead him out into the pasture. Jacob was confused. Maybe it was something that had fallen out of his pocket, or a little medallion he kept pinned to a fence somewhere. Kimball walked through the grass with Jacob trailing behind him, evidently with a destination in mind.

"Here we are," Kimball said proudly, far sooner than Jacob expected.

Jacob looked around. "Is it . . . I'm sorry, sir, but if you meant to get something from Blaze's saddlebags I think those are already in your house."

"No, no. Not the saddlebags. I want you to have Blaze."

"A horse? No, I—"

"You already agreed to take the gift," Kimball said with a teasing glint in his eye. "You can't let me down now, son."

"Aw, now, don't put it like that." Jacob backed up a couple steps. The truth was, he and Blaze had bonded more quickly than any of the other horses he had looked at since his own was shot. If he had been forced to go after that wild gang with Bonnie's horse, who knew what kind of disaster might have struck. Jacob already loved Blaze, and did indeed want to take him home. But surely this was too much. "Don't you need him?"

Kimball smiled. "Not hardly. With all the young ones around, he doesn't get near enough exercise. You'd be doing both me and Blaze a favor. He's a mustang, Jacob. Teaming up with a man like you would be the best thing for him."

"Well, but . . ." Jacob dithered. "At least let me buy him from you, Mr. Kimball. I got a sack of cash in my bag that's just been waiting till I found the right horse to invest in. I wouldn't feel right taking such a gorgeous creature free of charge."

"It's not free of charge, Jacob Payne." Kimball gently punched Jacob in the arm. "Didn't I tell you I offered a bounty on any man who could bring my daughter back safe and sound to me?"

"You did not." Jacob grinned in spite of himself.

"Sure, I did. Exactly the cost of one mustang named Blaze. Although, I suppose now that he's yours you can change his name if you see fit."

"I wouldn't change such a fine name for a fine horse."

"Ah-ha!" Kimball said triumphantly. "You admit you're going to accept him."

"I mean, I—"

"Give an old man like me something, Jacob. The best way I know to protect my daughter is to provide for the man who did. Blaze is yours."

Jacob let out a slow breath before nodding. "All right, Mr. Kimball. I . . . I won't fight you. Blaze will come home with me."

"And if you do come back up to Elk Springs, be sure to send word out here so I can come see him."

"Will do, sir."

ALSO BY A.T. BUTLER

Courage On The Oregon Trail Series:

Westward Courage

Faithful Trail

Frontier Sisters

Unyielding Heart

Wild Promise

Fierce Dreams

Jacob Payne, Bounty Hunter Series:

Trouble By Any Name

Danger in the Canyon

Justice for Jasper

Blood on the Mountain

Outlaw Country

Death By Grit

Desert Rage

Arizona Legend

Fool's Demise

Silent Night

Bountiful Justice Series:

Loyalty's Price

Riding for Justice

Trail of Redemption

Other Western Novels by A.T. Butler:

Hawke's Revenge

ABOUT THE AUTHOR

I grew up in the southwest—California Missions, snakes and constant threat of drought weaving the backdrop of my childhood.

But it wasn't until I moved to Texas a few years ago that the magic and mythology of the American West began to seep into my soul.

I'd love to write western adventures for a long time.

If you enjoyed this book, a review on your favorite retailer would be greatly appreciated.

- A

Jacob Payne, Bounty Hunter: Books 1 - 4 is a work of fiction. Names, characters, places and incidents either are the product of the author's imagination or are used fictitiously. Any resemblance to actual persons living or dead, events or locales is entirely coincidental.

Copyright 2021 by A.T. Butler

All rights reserved.

No part of this publication may be reproduced, distributed, or transmitted in any form or by any means, including photocopying, recording or other electronic or mechanical methods, without the prior written permission of the publisher, except in the case of brief quotations embodied in critical reviews and certain other noncommercial uses permitted by copyright law.

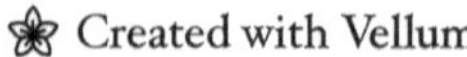 Created with Vellum